The Queen of Life

A Medieval Fantasy

Paul R. Cooper

The Queen of Life

ISBN 978-0-9896014-3-6

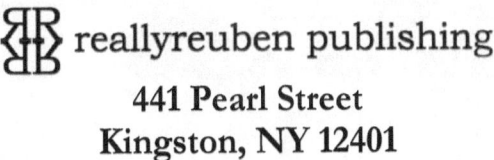

reallyreuben publishing

441 Pearl Street

Kingston, NY 12401

Foreword

The poet Marianne Moore famously wrote that poetry is “imaginary gardens with real toads in them.” Without claiming that this fantasy of mine is poetry, I’d like to say that for me, the kingdom of Grandlandia is my own imaginary garden wherein, I hope, the “real toads” are those human aspirations and dreams relevant not only to past times, but to our own.

Acknowledgements

This book has benefited from the helpful suggestions of my good friends Victor Caruso and Barbara Elsborg.

It was made *possible* by the unfailing encouragement and support of my dear wife, Carol, who makes *all* things possible for me.

For Carol

The Queen of Life

ONE
A Big Boy

Damian Agright thought himself a very big boy. He was all of eight years old, quite tall for his age, and strong enough to pick up his father's sword (though he needed two hands to do it). But when standing next to that man-mountain, Lord John Flexner, Damian felt tiny, and it took all his courage to say: "General Flexner, may I ask you a question?"

"Of course, young man," Lord John rumbled. "Ask away."

Young Damian drew himself up to his full height of 50 inches. "Is it true that with only one hand on your sword you can cut a man in half just like *that?"* said Damian, snapping his fingers with an impressive crack. This brought a slight smile to the lips of his escort, Lady Prudence Alder, who had observed him continually practicing this snap on the way over.

But Lord John took the question very seriously. "Young man ..." the General began, then trailed off, deep in thought. He had been asked that question seemingly at least once a day since the rebellion had been put down. In all that time he had been able to come up with but one satisfactory reply: "I can only say," he continued out loud, "that what I have done, I've done for my Queen. I hope she won't need it again, but if she does, I'm ready."

Flexner inclined his huge frame towards the boy, perhaps realizing that his reply was rather stiff for someone of any age, let alone for an eight-year-old, and he said, very gently, "Do you get my drift?"

"Yes *sir!*" said Damian, jumping to attention and saluting.

"Good lad!" said the General, saluting in return. "But did you come to the Fair simply to ask me this?"

Damian seemed tongue-tied, so Lady Prudence spoke up: "Of course not, Lord John. He didn't know you'd be at the Fair; nobody did. But when he saw you, he wanted to ask his question – he's been practicing it now for a week. I thought if he got it out of his system it might be best for everyone."

"Indeed," said Flexner, inclining again toward the little boy. "And what is your name, young man?"

"Damian Agright!" said the little one loudly, almost defiantly.

"Agright?!" The General began to glower.

Lady Prudence stepped forward, as if to protect the lad. Taller than most women, she provided for Damian a comforting shield against the man-mountain. "It's all right, Lord Flexner. Damian's not the oldest son, so he doesn't have to be in the Compound."

"Of course not; I wasn't thinking."

"He's been through enough," Prudence said; "there's no need to afflict him further."

"I'm sure you're right," said Lord Flexner, who looked closely at Damian and saw that the boy was staring at the ground, his feet pawing at it like some of the animals penned at the Fair. "Too much talk, eh, my lad?" he said. "Why not go off and take a look. You're a big boy, and if Lady Prudence gives you permission, you can go by yourself."

"Oh may I please, Aunt Prudence?" The boy fairly quivered with eagerness.

"Yes you may - but don't go far. Make sure you can always see us - all right?"

Damian didn't reply right away, so General Lord Flexner said, "Your Aunt Prudence is your commanding officer. How should you reply to her?"

"Yes, *my Lady!*" Damian cried, and ran off to take a look at the teams of draft oxen whose respective owners had arranged a contest to see which team could out-pull the others.

Lord Flexner gave Prudence a speculative look. "I didn't know you were related to the Agrights," he said.

"I'm not," she said, "but Lady Agright is a friend of mine. She's due to deliver at any moment—"

"Still breeding are they?" Flexner interrupted. "That's the last thing this country needs."

"I don't know enough to comment on that," said Prudence, coolly, "but I *can* say that an active, energetic eight-year-old - no matter who they've got to take care of him - is not what they need in that household right now. I volunteered to take him off their hands because it's not every day I get to keep company with a young person. She's doing *me* a kindness."

Flexner looked downcast. "Forgive me. I spoke out of turn."

She gave him an inquiring look. "You do seem not so buoyant as you usually are at the Castle, My Lord; in fact, you seem quite out of sorts, today."

"I may well *be*. And for today's errand," he said, "out of sorts is the last thing I need to be."

"You have to be in a good mood to acquire livestock for your place?"

"I'm not acquiring livestock – except in a manner of speaking. I have been ordered – by Her Majesty – to come here and find ... a wife."

"For yourself?"

"Yes, for myself unfortunately, though I'd scarcely be able to find a woman for anyone else. I fear I'm backward in this sort of thing; Her Majesty knows it, so she suggests places I might go to find someone suitable."

"I take it you've made little progress."

"None."

"Well, perhaps you'll see someone intriguing today – right here."

"Lady Alder," he said, staring down at the ground, "I don't see a blessed thing."

"Well, look up! Look around; you'll never see anything if you don't look."

"I *have* looked, I tell you, and I've seen nothing."

Prudence herself could see in the milling crowds at least three very winsome, nubile young women, suitably escorted by their parents for the very purpose of advertising their availability to eligible bachelors. And if they did encounter someone promising there was plenty to begin conversation – the cloudless sky, the exquisitely manicured topiary, and of course, if all else failed, the animals. There was plenty to see – but Prudence became aware that General Flexner was still talking:

"It's been almost a year since I got the order," he said, "and Her Majesty keeps pressing me. I'm afraid that soon she may run out of patience and choose someone herself. Then the fat would be in the fire. Having no one to talk to is bad enough, I can tell you, but having the *wrong* one would be a lot worse, I'm quite sure."

Prudence gave him a probing glance. "Her Majesty is very smart," she said. "How can you be sure she would make a bad choice?"

"Because at this stage *any* choice would be a bad one; from my point of view there *is* no good choice, period."

"Dare I ask why?" asked Prudence, who thought she already knew the answer. She took her courage in her hands and asked, "Is your heart already given?"

Flexner looked away for a few moments, but just as she was mustering the courage to apologize for invading his privacy, he turned and looked her full in the face. "That's it," he said, firmly.

"And may I know who's the lucky woman?" asked Prudence, who by now had guessed who she was.

"She knows who she is, but that doesn't help things. She is dead set against marrying anyone. If I am married off, that takes pressure off *her*. Need I say more?"

It was not necessary to say more. General Lord Flexner had just confirmed the gossiping surmise of everyone in the realm – that his loyal devotion to his Queen had grown into a romantic obsession that would not, *could* not be requited. He turned away from Prudence, and could not see her pitying look. "And the thing is," he said, "Her Majesty won't be satisfied until I have a child – preferably a son. But even if I found someone I liked, the chances of my wife surviving childbirth would be next to nil."

"But why?"

"Look at me, my Lady," said the man-mountain.

She did. "Oh," she said. She saw that he was blushing, and looked away, blushing too. "We can't *know* these things," she murmured. "We can only guess, and sometimes we guess wrong. But still ..." *He may never have children,* she thought. *O God, a life without children* ... "Children!" she cried out. "Oh my God – Damian! I don't see him! He's gone!"

"Don't panic, my Lady," said Flexner, "we'll find him." And he ran toward where the oxen competition was about to start, and he shouted, "Damian! Damian!" But Damian was nowhere to be found. So with nimbleness astonishing in someone so huge, the man-mountain vaulted onto a brace of oxen, yoked together. He bestrode them both and bellowed, "Damian Agright: *FALL IN!"* And the eight-year-old sheepishly emerged from a horse stall where he had been hiding. By that time Prudence had caught up with them. She knelt and hugged Damian hard enough almost to squeeze the breath out of him.

"Oh, Damian," she said, "never do that again! Promise me that you'll never scare us that way again."

"What do you say to your commanding officer, Agright?" Flexner loomed over them both like a massive tower of justice, seeming to eclipse half the sky. "Tell me, Agright, what do you say to her?"

"I promise, my Lady," Damian murmured.

"You had better mean it," said Flexner.

"I do ... I do ... but don't tell my father. Please!"

"You keep your word, Agright, and he'll never hear it from *me*."

Still kneeling and hugging Damian, Prudence looked up at Flexner and said, "I fear our conversation has ended prematurely, My Lord."

"Perhaps we can resume it, some time."

"I'd like that."

But Damian was pawing the ground impatiently, and Prudence noticed. "Are you never going to give us a moment's rest?" she asked. "It's getting toward your supper time; I've got to get you home. Then your governess can take care of you, and I can recover."

Flexner laughed. "Don't take too long recovering, my Lady. Apparently there are many who depend on you."

TWO

You are not to wave back – ever.

Lady Abigail Agright asked her handmaid to prop up her pillows and help her sit up in bed. That done, she turned to Prudence. "I really should be up and dressed and managing things," she told her. "But since I lost the last baby, His Lordship won't hear of it. He almost didn't allow you to spend the afternoon with Damian – all this political nonsense, you understand."

"Yes, I do understand, my Lady," Prudence murmured.

"But I told that husband of mine that if he didn't allow you to take care of Damian this afternoon, I would get out of bed and see to my responsibilities myself, right away, and if they tried to hold me down as he threatened, and if I miscarried, then it would be his fault and not mine."

"My Lady, try not to upset yourself," said Prudence. "Everything will be all right."

"Prudence, my love, what would we do without you? Thank you so much for taking Damian off our hands this afternoon – you're a godsend."

"It was my pleasure. He has splendid energy, and is a very dear lad. You're lucky to have him."

"Oh, you're such a lovely person," said Lady Abigail, reaching for Prudence's hand and kissing it. Then she sighed and sank back into the pillows.

"I fear I'm tiring you," said Prudence, leaning over to kiss Abigail's forehead. "Do get some sleep, tonight, my

Lady, and I'll come round tomorrow to see if there's anything more I can do."

Already half asleep, Abigail murmured, "Good night, my Lady."

Unlike Lady Abigail, Prudence was not descended from nobility but was called "My Lady" as a courtesy, since she was an old friend to the Queen, to whom she was First Lady-In-Waiting. Lady Abigail, in contrast, stemmed from exceedingly aristocratic forebears, and would have been called "My Lady" even had she not married Albemarle Agright, the Viscount of Domeny. And so Prudence curtsied to her and made her way out of Lady Abigail's personal bed-chamber. She went downstairs, and started walking through the baronial Great Room.

She had not been concerned about meeting the Viscount in Her Ladyship's room upstairs, since it was well known by the household staff that Lord Albemarle never visited that room except for what he termed "dynastic purposes." But on her way out of the mansion she did encounter him. "Good evening, Your Lordship," she said, and he nodded curtly. Seeing Damian with him, she waved to the lad, and he waved back happily.

Lord Agright spoke up: "I know I need not have anyone see you out, Mistress Alder," he growled; "you've been here enough times."

"Good night, sir," she said, and departed, leaving the Viscount and his younger son alone together.

Lord Agright turned to Damian. "I don't care how many times that woman waves to you," he said, "you are not to wave back. Ever."

"But she is my friend."

"No. She is a friend to the Queen, which means that she can never be a friend to our family."

"Why?"

"There'll be time enough for you to understand – when you're older. Right now, all you have to remember is that your older brother, the next Viscount, is in a prison compound near the Castle Royal, and that the Queen put him there."

"Why did she?"

"I've told you why a hundred times; when will you understand? She did it to make me walk on eggshells lest she harm Emanuel. Do you get it now?"

Damian wasn't sure he got it. He knew that his father never referred to the Queen as her Majesty; it was always "The Queen," or "that woman," or – if he thought Damian was out of earshot – "that bitch."

Repeatedly Damian had asked his mother what was behind all this, and all she would say was, "your father is the head of the house, and while he shelters us under his roof, we are to follow his lead, and not ask why."

"Are you listening to me?" said the Viscount. "Do you understand what I just said?" A thin smile had wormed its way onto his face, and he was speaking with insidious quiet: "Or perhaps you too want to become an enemy to your family?"

"No, no, I don't want ... I don't want ..." said the boy, starting to cry.

"Don't cry. Don't cry, for heaven's sake! I know you're no enemy," said the Viscount, at last starting to soften. "You're really too young to understand these things. You're just a little boy."

"I'm not a little boy," said Damian, blubbering.

"You're a child of my old age, that's what you are, and what little boys need is hugging and kissing." And the Viscount imprisoned Damian in his arms, and ran his hand through the boy's thatch of brown hair. You know I love you – right? *Right?*"

"Yes, father," Damian murmured.

"Good. You're too young to worry about the family's honor. That's what fathers are for – to take care of things. And take care of them I will. Believe me: I know how to get even."

Viscount Agright looked away from his young son, grimaced, and then said quietly: "It's what I do best." Unconsciously, he fingered the solid gold bracelet on his left wrist. Soldered to the bracelet was the family crest of which he was so proud: the Agright coat of arms, which told – as far as he was concerned – the whole story.

THREE

A chess game, is it?

Dominating Queen Anna's Council Room was an outsized, rough-hewn oak table covered with purple cloth on which was embroidered, in gold thread, the Royal Coat of Arms, with its two Lions Rampant. And resting on that purple cloth was a cherry wood casket which had been covered in crimson velvet before Anna removed it.

"What kind of joke is this?!" cried Anna, her face pale. She had opened the casket and was gazing incredulously at its contents.

"Joke, your Majesty?" said the Vicomte de la Rocheaimard, his mustachios oiled and pointed. "My master meant no joke; he couldn't have been more sincere. To influence you to consider seriously his offer of marriage, His Majesty, François, whom they call 'The Great,' has sent you a portrait of himself."

Anna turned to the Vicomte with barely concealed exasperation. "But this cannot be a portrait of King François of France."

"And why not, your Majesty?"

"Because it is a picture of the late Lord Andrew Steele, Baron of Bellemont, may God rest his soul. He was the man who would have been my consort had he not been killed in the recent rebellion. And to toy with my heart, King François would send me *this? **It is not amusing!***" By this time, Anna had raised her voice to such a pitch that everyone in the room was dumbfounded.

General Lord Flexner was transfixed by her. The color had flooded back into her cheeks, and her eyes were flashing. He had never seen her more beautiful.

He turned away. He could no more gaze at Anna, he felt, than he could gaze at the sun. Her abundance of auburn hair, which when Andrew Steele was alive she had allowed to cascade down to her shoulders, was now neatly coiffed, so that it merely hinted at the riches that would overspread the pillow of the man lucky enough to bed her. *Oh God, I can't go on like this,* he thought, *I must get a grip!*

He saw that Anna had certainly regained *her* outward composure. She turned calmly to Rocheaimard. "Where did you get this?" she asked quietly.

"As I told you, Your Majesty, my liege lord the King gave it me."

"And where did *he* get it?"

"The Court Artist made it."

"Forgive me, My Lord, I but don't believe you." Anna reached into the casket with both hands and gingerly lifted the portrait – drawn on a slab of wood – and held it to the window's light. "This image is Lord Andrew to the life," she said. "The cut of that beard, the strength of that mouth and that brow – they're in my dreams! If an image could bring a loved one back to life, this one would. But no: Three years ago we laid Andrew's body in the coffin, just as we now lay this ... this *outrage* back in the box where it belongs. Do not trouble us any further with it, or with your master's protestations of love." Anna turned her back on the casket, and said to Lord Turco, "What is keeping that sister of mine? Are you sure you sent for Her Royal Highness as I asked you?"

"Absolutely, ma'am," said Turco. "Shall I go fetch her myself?"

"No need for that," said Princess Jane, entering the Council Room. "I came as fast as I could. Now what is all this fuss and fury?"

"Jane," said Anna, "there's a picture inside that box on the table. We'd like you to look and tell us if you drew it."

"Certainly," said the Princess, who made her way over to the casket and looked inside. "Oh! Very interesting!" she said, "and impressive – in its way. But it's not my work." She reached into the casket, and then paused. "May I?"

The Queen nodded.

Jane lifted the picture out of the casket with one hand, while the other gestured toward it to make her point: "This isn't my style. I go for the long, incisive line which suggests a lot with a little. The person who drew this has a crabbed style; I mean he carefully copies each external feature with lots of little marks. I outgrew that years ago. Don't get me wrong, this artist knows what he's doing, and he's captured an external likeness. But I haven't drawn like that since I was eight." Whereupon Jane replaced the picture in its cherry wood casket.

"Dear Jane, think back," said Anna. "Do you think you could have drawn Lord Andrew as a small child, when you did draw like that?"

"Not really. When I was that age, the only one I wanted to draw was Sir Turco – Lord Turco, now. In those days it took me a long time to do each picture – and Sir Turco was the only one with the patience to sit for me."

"But you *did* draw Lord Andrew. You told me you had."

"And I did – on Monument Mountain, a few days before the battle. And sometime after the funeral, I told you about the picture; I thought you might want it. And you told me that you couldn't bear to see it, and that as far as you were concerned, I could get rid of it. So I did."

"You what?!"

"The French Envoy wanted to buy it from me; I didn't need the money, so I just gave it to him."

"Aha! That explains everything!"

"Explains what?"

"Princess Jane, you may thank God you don't have to put up with what we have to. Listen to this: To tempt us into marriage with him, King François of France – who calls himself 'The Great' – claims that this is his very own likeness, drawn at Court. How pathetic! Did he suppose that once he arrived we wouldn't be able to tell the difference?"

The Vicomte de la Rocheaimard spoke up: "I am here to tell you, your Majesty, that when his Majesty King François does arrive, you will not be able to tell the difference, because there will *be* none. I will wager my life on it."

"You wager your life very easily, My Lord."

"When you see his Majesty, you will understand why."

"You seem confident that we will invite that jokester here."

"He is no jokester, and I am confident you will invite him, because you are a woman not only of beauty, but of peace. And it is peace and love that my master offers. With all humility, I suggest that you would do well to consider his offer, rather than reject my liege lord out of hand. He would not swallow that easily, I can tell you."

"Did your liege lord authorize you to say that? It sounds to us like a threat."

"His Majesty threatens nothing but everlasting peace and amity between our two nations."

"By his nation subsuming ours? That sort of peace and amity we Grandlandians can do without."

"It pleases you to be light, your Majesty."

"Enough!" cried Anna. "Monsieur le Vicomte, when do you return to France?"

"Tomorrow at dawn, your Majesty. My Captain advises me that wind and tides will be most favorable then."

"In the morning, before you set out, you will have your answer. In the meantime, we bid you good night, My Lord."

"Good night, your Majesty." And the Vicomte de la Rocheaimard bowed and backed out of the room, leaving Queen Anna with her advisors.

"He can't leave soon enough for me," said Count Edgar of Ravenshead. "What sort of man is this liege lord of his who – *knowing* that Your Majesty is still in mourning, and, he supposes, vulnerable – would have the gall to present himself as a *replacement* for the love you have lost? He's either supremely egotistical, or utterly dismissive of women as being weak and easily seduced, or – more charitably – just someone hopelessly tasteless."

"How about all three?" said Anna the Queen. "Propose any insult for King François, and I'll subscribe to it."

She pointed to the cherry-wood casket. "Will someone cover that thing?" she said, whereupon Count Edgar of Ravenshead, without a word, sprang up and draped the velvet crimson over the casket, which seemed to scream its presence all the more loudly for its being hidden. For a few moments, Anna stared at it, while no one dared move. Finally, she took her eyes away and cleared her throat. “What was I saying?”

Count Edgar spoke up: “You were saying that you’d subscribe to any insult for King François.”

“Well of course,” Anna said. “There is no doubt in my mind that his romantic purpose is to subjugate me and the entire country. If he were to set foot on our soil, his footsteps would pollute the realm.”

“I agree completely!” came the rumble of that man-mountain, General Lord John Flexner. “He is a scoundrel. I pity the French.”

“Then you agree that I should reject him out of hand?”

“That should be studied,” said Lord Turco of Pleasantvale. “The man does mean to conquer us. Seducing Your Majesty - from *his* point of view - would be ideal, entailing minimal losses for the French, and maximum pleasure for him. But if you reject him now, you give him an excuse immediately to mount an armada which will assault our shores within months - perhaps even sooner. That, I believe, was what his envoy was hinting.”

“Are we prepared for that, General Flexner?”

“I think so, ma’am; I believe we are ready now, and by the time his forces get here, I’ll be more certain of it.”

“The one thing we lack,” said Turco, “is full knowledge of our enemy. Other than he is a dastard, we don’t know that much about him.”

“We can guess fairly well.” said Anna.

"Yes, we can. But with all due respect, ma'am, guessing fairly well isn't as good as *knowing.*"

"So what are you saying, Lord Turco?"

"I'm saying that we should consider inviting François here, to give him the impression that Your Majesty is not ill-disposed to his proposal. Without expressing it in so many words, you could give him the sense that your cautious heart is moved almost to melting by his physical being, but needs to be a little more sure that this is the right thing for both your countries. By giving him the impression that he is disarming you, you will be disarming *him.*"

"But won't he be on guard against this?" Anna said. "Won't he be *looking* for signs of duplicity on our part?"

"If he's smart, of course he will, ma'am, and he'll be looking to ferret out useful strategic information from you, just as you will be looking for the same from him. But judging by the gift in that box, I doubt he's all that smart. In all likelihood, you're a lot smarter than King Frenchy – which will stand you in good stead in this chess game."

The man-mountain visibly darkened. "A chess game, is it?"

"Something very much like that. For our side, our most powerful player will indeed be our Queen. Which means that we must be careful to guard her from danger until the right moment, when she makes her move."

"Whatever that means," Flexner growled. "Will all due respect to you, Lord Turco, what you propose is dangerous. It's hard to believe that an advisor to Her Majesty would give such counsel."

"It *is* unexpected," said Turco, "which is one of the reasons it just might work. But you are quite right: My plan *is* dangerous – no doubt about it. The truth is Her Majesty is already in great danger even now, as we speak. François' covetous eyes are on our little country, and his ultimate aim is to get rid of Her Majesty so he can swallow up Grandlandia, make serfs of us all, and dominate us without any restraint whatsoever. France is more than three times our size, with more than thrice our resources. In a protracted head-to-head confrontation, they could simply wear us down, till we had nothing left to fight with. What to do? While I am not the military student that you are, My Lord, I have heard that fooling the enemy with an adroit feint can sometimes work wonders."

"But how do you know François will fall for it?" said Ravenshead.

"I *don't* know. But consider the gift that he sent Her Majesty – a picture of himself. That could mean that he is self-absorbed at the very least. And if so, his vanity would make him *want* to fall for it. This could give us the edge we need."

There was a brief silence, as if everyone were waiting for Anna the Queen to pronounce, definitively, her reaction to Turco's idea. If so, they didn't have to wait long. "Lord Turco," said Anna at last, this is the sort of thinking I had thought never to hear again, after Lord Andrew was taken from us. But in this latest idea of yours, you have almost equaled him."

"During my life," said Turco, "I have received many compliments – most of them undeserved. But the compliment you have given me just now, ma'am, is the greatest compliment of all – and the least merited."

Anna the Queen replied, "that remains to be seen. In the meantime, if everyone will excuse us, we need to be alone with General Flexner."

So the rest of them bowed and backed out of her presence, leaving her alone with Lord John, upon whom she might have to depend once again for the realm's very existence, not to mention her own.

FOUR

The sword of danger has two edges.

General Flexner and Queen Anna were still sitting at the large, rough-hewn oak table, she at its head, and he close to her, but around the corner as it were, at the table's long side. The velvet-covered casket remained on the table – a crimson presence, glowing.

Anna regarded Flexner gravely. "Tell me your thoughts, My Lord," she said quietly.

"Majesty, Lord Turco is a very clever man - more clever than I by half. But it takes no cleverness to know that François means to kill you. His project is total domination of Grandlandia, which he cannot have so long as you're alive."

"I know that."

"Then why invite him here and make his project easier, and my job harder – which is to protect you?"

"Because the sword of danger has two edges."

"Ma'am?"

"What I mean is that I will not be the only one in danger. King François will be away from home, and whatever cohort he brings with him will be no match for our forces, who *know* where they are. Great as he thinks he is, *he* may be the one to fall - by my hand, if necessary."

"By *your hand?!*"

"What's the matter? You think I can't fight?"

Everyone at Court knew that the late King Edgar tried to teach his little Anna the rudiments of self defense, those lessons stopping when Edgar was killed in battle.

There were no such lessons during the reign of his widow Queen Thanata, who kept the Princesses Anna and Jane virtual prisoners in the Castle. Thanata's suicide freed the sisters, but their happiness was short lived, the rebellion breaking out the day after Anna was crowned. Anna was not able to resume regular practice until the rebellion finally was put down, allowing Anna and her Trainer to begin working out with wooden swords in the court yard.

Flexner had seen them doing it once or twice, and had noted how earnestly she worked at it. But more than that, he marveled at her lithe athleticism -- she seemed to have a body that could do anything that she or a lover – he imagined – could ask of it. But earnest sword practice does not a warrior make, and she had a duty to her country *to be careful.* How to tell her?

"Your Majesty," he began, "we all mourned the loss of His Majesty your father, and we all revere his memory. But I have to say that he was less than prudent, putting himself in the front lines, leading by fighting at the head of all the troops, and *they*, one day, had to watch him being hacked to pieces! One of the first rules of a King should be, *let your armies do your fighting for you.* He either forgot that, or maybe he had something to prove. If so, he proved it all right!"

"What are you saying? Be respectful!" There was high color in Anna's face.

"Forgive me, Your Majesty, but I want you alive! Despite what Turco says, this is not a game of chess; it's the real thing! And if – God forbid – we should lose our Queen, it isn't just 'game over' – it's '*life* over' as far as

I'm concerned." Tears were welling up in his eyes, and he looked away.

But Anna the Queen didn't have to see his face to know what he was feeling. She leaned toward him and put her hand over his. "How's the wife search coming, My Lord?" she asked.

He snapped his head around. "What's that got to do with your risking your life?"

"You no longer answer your Queen?"

"Forgive me, Majesty. What was the question?"

"How's the wife search coming?"

"Oh! Well ... *that* thing ... I've been looking ... went to the Fair the other day ..."

"Any luck?"

"Not really. But – may I be candid with you, Your Majesty?"

"Of course. From my General I expect nothing but candor."

"Well then, with your permission, ma'am, may I say that ... what with the clouds of war gathering over our little country, this seems to be the wrong time to talk of love."

"My dear Lord, it's never the wrong time to talk of love. Not in this, or in any other place I want to imagine. I hope Grandlandia will be where everyone can know love as their first priority – if they want it to be. That can only happen if the country is secure enough. That's where you come in."

"Yes, ma'am, I know it. And I know also that if I were to find someone to marry, it would take a burden off you."

"Don't think of it that way. Think of marriage as a delight. Think of it as being with someone to whom you belong and who belongs to you alone. That would be someone *unlike me*, who belongs to the nation alone. I want to give you the joy I never can have myself – except through people I care for. If you want to give me that joy, then please don't stop looking for a bride."

After a brief pause to collect his thoughts, Flexner said, "I'm still looking, ma'am. And at the Fair I did happen to run into Prudence – Lady Alder. She's very sensible. Much more than I am in these things. I was thinking of having her help me look."

"Lady Alder is indeed very sensible," said Anna the Queen. "I'm sure she'll help you."

FIVE

That sounds like a threat.

That night, the first warning to Albemarle Agright, Viscount of Domeny, was the deep throated barking of his bull mastiffs, alerting him that some stranger was on the estate. Luckily for the stranger, the dogs were kept inside. Also inside was Benedict, Agright's venerable Chamberlain, who came hastily into the Viscount's study.

"My Lord! My Lord!" he said, a bit out of breath, "there's someone knocking at the door. I've never seen him before."

"Get rid of him," said the Viscount, "it's too late for an honest visitor." But as Benedict turned to go, Agright said, "Wait a minute – a *dis*honest visitor might prove interesting. Was there anyone with him?"

"Not that I could see, My Lord."

"All right. Get some guards – four of them will do – and let them escort our interesting visitor here to my study. We'll find out his business."

And soon enough, escorted by four heavily armed guards, a small, slight man appeared in the Viscount's study. He looked to be about thirty years old, and his tousled hair and disheveled clothes suggested he had walked a great distance under the moonlight, but had elected not to travel by main roads – such as they were.

"All right, sirrah," said Agright, "Who are you, and what is your business?"

"May I approach, My Lord?" the little man asked. Agright nodded, and the stranger took a few steps toward him until the Viscount signaled him to stop.

"That's far enough," he said.

"My Lord, We need to speak alone."

"Oh, do we now?" Agright's eyebrow arched up. "And why, pray?"

The stranger gestured with his head to indicate the four guards behind him, and with a quiet voice, spoke evenly: "If you want me to help you realize your deepest desire, they must go."

Agright thought a bit, then pulled out of its sheath a small dagger that he always carried with him. He held it up so that the little man could see it. "This is extremely sharp," he said, and I'm very good with it; do you follow me?"

"My Lord, I do."

"All right then." He looked at his guards and said: "It's all right for you to leave me alone with this man. Go outside and close the door behind you. Then wait outside the door. If you hear anything suspicious, barge right in. Do you understand?"

"Yes, My Lord," they chorused, then left the two men alone as they had been instructed.

"Now then," said Agright, "what's your story?"

The little man said, in a very low voice, "I arrived here on the *Bonhomme Marcel, and I—*"

"The Viscount's ship!" The exclamation was almost a shout.

The stranger lifted a delicate finger to his lips, and drew much closer to Agright. Then, almost in a whisper, he said "Be careful, My Lord," he said. "Let us pray that none of those guards outside heard you. The safety of your family, the success of my project, not to mention the fulfillment of your deepest desire, all depend upon secrecy – and your discretion."

"All right," Agright said with quiet intensity, if you've arrived on that ship, you're from France, correct? So how the hell do you know my deepest desire?"

"*Mon cher,*" said the little man, "everyone knows it, *tout le monde!* The whole world knows what it is: The one who wears this ..." and the stranger mimed the placing of a crown on his own head, "gets *this:* ... " and using his thumb to represent a knife, drew his thumb across his neck, while the features of his face contorted to suggest his choking on the blood pouring out of his mouth. This grisly performance lasted about ten seconds, after which he mimed the removing of the crown from his head, setting it on the Viscount's table. Then, interlacing his slender fingers, he rested his hands in his lap and smiled insouciantly. "Am I clear?"

"You couldn't be clearer," said Agright, "and nothing could more satisfy my deepest desire – except perhaps to see it with my own eyes."

"All that in due time. Patience, *mon oncle.* All I need from you is five pounds of silver, so I can begin my project, and then I'll disappear."

Agright frowned. "I don't give away five pounds of silver unless I know what they're going to be spent on."

"It is not to be advised. If they torture you, you want to be able to tell them truthfully that you don't know."

"I'll take that chance. Tell me," said the Viscount, "what is the money *for?*"

"His Majesty King François is soon to set foot on your fair country. But before he does, he would like to know the lay of the land, so to speak."

"You mean location of roads, mountains, lakes - that sort of thing?"

"Well - that is always useful knowledge, and in time, we'll need it. But more important, right now, is his Majesty's need to ascertain if there still are pockets of resentment against Queen Anna, and if so, *where* they are."

"Right now I can tell you where one huge pocket of resentment is!"

"*Oui, mon cher Vicomte*, but *tout le monde* knows that. What I'm to find out is who - besides yourself - harbors bitter feelings against Her Majesty. You are obvious; others may be less so."

Agright's eyes narrowed. "How do I know you're not an agent of the Queen? That would be very clever of that witch - to dress you up as a foreign agent - with French accent and all - to ferret out from me details of any remaining resistance. How can I be absolutely certain you haven't come straight from the Castle Royal?"

"*Mon cher*, nothing is absolutely certain in this life - except the leaving of it. You have a right to your suspicions. And if I started asking you questions, you'd certainly be entitled to them. But I ask you no questions."

"Then how will you learn where your sympathizers are? And *who* they are?"

"That's my business; it's better that you don't know it, and that nobody even *thinks* you know. I'm sure you're aware of the danger to Emanuel if your name should be connected to my doings."

"I'm very aware of it. But how do you know my son's name?"

"It's best you not know."

"May I know *your* name?"

"I have many ... and you need not know any of them."

"In the future, how I will address you?"

"With any luck," said the stranger, "we won't meet again, and you won't need to address me. Right now, all you need know is that with those five pounds of silver you're going to give me, you are going to do King François a big favor, and in time you will learn that Sa Majesté knows how to thank people like you."

"His thanks are welcome, of course, but the thanks I most desire is the death of that bitch."

The little man raised an eyebrow. "And the safety of both your sons – Emanuel and Damian – don't forget *them*. I notice you wear a gold bracelet with your coat of arms. But what good is a family crest with no children to carry it forward?"

"That sounds like a threat."

"Mon cher Vicomte, why would we threaten you?"

"To ensure my compliance."

"Morbleu! Are you suggesting that our benevolent *Majesté* François is capable of so ruthless a thing?"

Suddenly, in the fortress of his own home with a dagger in his hand and four heavily armed guards outside the door, Albemarle Agright, Viscount of Domeny, felt very vulnerable. He spoke carefully: "I suggest nothing of the kind. I just don't want to misunderstand you."

"I'm glad," said the stranger, tapping his delicate fingers together. "Please have patience, *mon cher Vicomte.* I assure you that in due time, all the good things – all the *right* things – will happen."

SIX

An Interesting Project

"Before I say anything more," Lord Flexner said to Lady Prudence Alder, "I need you to swear that you won't tell anyone else about it, not even Her Majesty."

"Not even Her Majesty?!" Prudence exclaimed – so loudly that Flexner glanced nervously around him. But he had already made sure there would be no one close enough to hear them, having chosen for their walk a road which went by pastures of young grass on either side, so that the only people visible would be a few shepherds and their flocks of sheep – too distant to be of concern.

All the same he lowered his voice when he replied, "That's right: Not even Her Majesty."

"But what if she asks me directly, am I to lie?"

That brought Flexner up short; his pace slowed to a full stop while he considered his answer. "If Her Majesty asks you directly, then of course you must tell her the truth. But short of that, don't volunteer it."

"I won't, I promise."

Flexner heaved a great sigh. Then he told Prudence about King François' mustachioed ambassador of romance, and about his bringing the velvet covered casket with its surprising contents, which caused an explosive reaction from Her Majesty, who vowed to invite the French King here for the sole purpose of having him die – by her own hand if necessary. "I couldn't believe my ears!" Flexner cried. "Her Majesty is willing to risk her life – and that of the country – on a personal confrontation! I urged her to let her subjects do her fighting for her; I reminded her of what happened to her poor father. I pointed out that this was no mere game of chess, that if the Queen fell, she would fall never to rise again."

"And what did she say to all this?"

"She asked me how my wife search was going - as if that were somehow related!"

Flexner turned away in exasperation, and could not see Prudence's quiet smile. When he turned back, she was ready with a gentle admonition: "Maybe she meant that if you had a love of your own - who belonged to you only, and not to the whole nation - you might not be quite so invested in what happened to *her*."

"Forgive me, Lady Alder, but that makes no sense!" The man-mountain stomped off to a rock wall and, placing his foot on it, leaned forward as if to examine the meadow that it bordered. "I love my country, Prudence, so how could I not care about its Queen? One goes with the other. I'm worried that if Her Majesty should lay eyes on this King François, and if he should look anything like the picture he sent her, she will lose her heart to him, and lose her country to him as well. Then where would we be?"

Prudence went up to him and placed a hand on his shoulder (she was one of the few women in Grandlandia tall enough to do that easily). "That does scant credit to Her Majesty," she said. "Surely she is proof against that!"

He turned to face her. "You can never be sure," he said. "You'd think that I myself would be proof against that sort of thing, but apparently I'm not. Whenever I'm away from the Castle Royal, and I see someone who reminds me even remotely of Her Majesty, my heart leaps up. It's crazy. I know she's no longer disguising herself and going out incognito; I've told her she shouldn't anymore, and to my best knowledge, she doesn't. I *know* all this. Still, I become very excited at the thought that it *might* be her - even though I know the chance that it could be is less than a rabbit's lasting in a lion's mouth. If I could feel that way, how much more might Her Majesty feel if she saw restored to her the beloved face she thought she had lost forever? She's only human!"

"You didn't say all this to Her Majesty, I presume."

"Certainly not!" he exclaimed, whereupon Prudence raised a hushing finger to her lips: A shepherd, crook in hand, had drawn near – possibly near enough to hear.

Silently they walked on at a quicker pace, until the shepherd was out of earshot.

"So," Prudence continued, "when she asked how was the wife search going, what *did* you say?"

"I said you told me you'd help me with it, since you were more adept at that sort of thing than I."

"But I said no such thing!"

"I know you didn't," he said quietly, looking down at the ground. Then he raised his eyes to her and said, sheepishly, "but I was hoping you *would*."

"Really, Lord John? You're so fixed on Her Majesty, how could *anyone* help you?"

That was exactly what he had been asking himself for many months, only to conclude he was beyond help. But he had promised Her Majesty he would make an honest effort.

"Please – I beg you."

She looked at him speculatively, wondering if this was the first time that he had begged for anything. She raised an eyebrow. "Hm ... it might prove an interesting project.

All right. Put yourself in my hands, My Lord, and we'll see what we can do."

SEVEN

Do something!

When Viscount Albemarle Agright learned that his favorite bird had returned, he lost no time in hurrying to the loft. "Susannah, you are my sweetheart, my heart's treasure," he cooed, using the same loving words he had offered to Lady Abigail when he was courting her, some twenty years ago.

He saw nothing incongruous in this. Back then, the exchange of loving words was all their care, but the intervening years had laid other cares upon them: Upon her was the responsibility of bearing and rearing of his children; even now she was in labor bearing him a third child, which hopefully would not only be a son, but would be strong enough to survive childbirth, unlike the previous one. He knew that Abigail would see to these responsibilities with all her strength, but he wondered whether lately that strength seemed to be waning. Yet he set aside such worries, for he too had responsibilities – the husbanding of the family's fortune and the planning of the family's future. And all this responsibility, in his mind, depended upon the consequences of his favorite bird's return.

He said to her, "you always come home to me, don't you darling, because you know I'll have some special treat for you. So here it is, my love, here it is." And with that, the Viscount poured into a dish a few grains of barley mixed into some chopped apple. Susannah immediately fell to, not in the least minding Agright's opening the container on her leg, and removing a miniscule scroll on which was written tiny characters. He proceeded to read them - *aloud* - as if the grey bird had any interest in her precious cargo: "'*Mon cher ami,* you were right about Anna: She is as *vulnérable* as you described - easy pickings for our King François. After it's all over, your reward will be handsome, and I will shake the hand of my fellow *Vicomte.*' And he signs it: Rocheaimard." He turned to the bird, who had just finished her special treat. "Not bad, eh?" -

How could it be bad? he kept asking himself. But with a sinking feeling, he thought of the mysterious, nameless caller that had visited him, not long ago, and the visitor's implied threat to his sons, Emanuel and Damian. And he wondered, why would so rich and powerful a King as François need to send his nameless spy, like a mendicant, to his door to ask him for a mere five pounds of silver? Obviously, the reason was not the money, but the need to ensnare him into the conspiracy, whether he wanted to be part of it or not. So what? He *did* want to be part of it, didn't he? So what harm was there in it? François *did* have a hold over him, but so what? All was still well, wasn't it? He tried to shake off the feeling that all might *not* be so well.

He offered his finger to Susannah, and the bird obediently climbed onto it. Then Agright said to her, "He speaks of handsome rewards, and if he happens to offer one, of course we'll accept it. But you and I know, don't we, my beauty, that whatever he can give me is superfluous. You cannot reward revenge, which is its own reward - nothing else comes close."

Once again, Agright congratulated himself on having the forethought to build on one of his many roofs a pigeon loft so secret that only he and his Chamberlain knew of its existence. Had it not been for this clandestine means of communication, the Queen's agents might long ago have divined his purpose - to bring down Her Majesty once and for all.

His musings were interrupted by the cry, "My Lord! My Lord! Come quickly – Her Ladyship needs you!" It was Agright's elderly retainer, Benedict, Chamberlain of the mansion.

"Did anyone see you come in here?" Agright demanded.

"No, My Lord – but Her Ladyship needs you."

"What? Has she given birth?"

"This way, My Lord – come quickly!"

Then, with speed unusual in such an ancient, Benedict led the way to Lady Abigail's bed chamber. Agright entered, only to have his eyes assailed with the sight of Abigail swathed in bandages, all soaked in blood.

"Oh my god - Abby!" He ran to her side and saw that her lips were moving. He bent down to her face, now like parchment, and heard her whisper, "Sorry ... so sorry ... take care of Damian." And with that she stopped breathing, though her eyes remained open.

He straightened, and looked around the room wildly. His eyes fastened on Prudence. "Do something!" he cried. With a look of great sadness and pity, she approached the bed side, as he backed away from it. Prudence took his place and closed Abigail's eyes. Then she turned to Agright, who was teetering as if the ground were shifting beneath him. "Why not sit down, My Lord?" she asked, gently.

"Don't touch me!"

"Steady, My Lord."

"Don't you come near me – or I'll show you a 'steady' you'll never forget. What happened to the baby?"

"Still born, My Lord."

"That too? Does the Queen have that too, to answer for?" he exclaimed in a rising voice, "***then so be it!***" He turned on his heel and walked to the door, then turned back to look at Prudence and snarled, "You do what you women do in these cases. Clean her up, get her ready. Arrange for the funeral, the burial. Let me know when they are."

And with that he stalked out of the bedchamber, went out the front door, and walked well away from the mansion. After a mile or so, the road entered deep woods – part of the vast holdings his family had held for hundreds of years. As a child he loved to play Soldier-Spy in these woods; as an adolescent he'd go there with the neighboring farm girls and play other games. But after he met Abigail, he tried – not altogether successfully – to put away such liaisons as not being worthy of Lady Abigail's future husband. Instead Lady Abigail and he would stroll through the woods on a path very much like the one he was now on, and they found a clearing not unlike the one he saw in front of him, except that this one was much more overgrown than the one he remembered. Well, why not – nothing stays the same forever! But look: In the middle of the clearing was an oak – similar to the one he remembered, although much bigger, of course. Was it the same tree? He had carved deeply into its bark two overlapping A's – one for Albemarle, the other for Abigail. Then, on the insignia thus made she placed her delicate white hand; he placed his much larger hand over hers, and they both vowed to love each other forever; they promised to return to the site once a year to renew their vows.

They never did. Their children, his business, *life* – got in the way. Was it the same tree? He walked around to the North side of the tree where he had gouged the trunk, but saw only moss. He took out his knife and started scraping the moss away; it *had* to be there! And then, in the fading light, he saw traces of the scars he had inflicted years ago. Very excited now, he placed his hand over them, trying to remember the feeling of her cool white hand under his, her flesh all silken. Tears sprang to his eyes, and he fell to his knees, racked with sobs.

EIGHT
A single red rose

The burial was a private affair, performed in the family graveyard located on the Viscount's estate. It was attended only by close friends and family. The elder son, Emanuel, was allowed out of the Compound to attend, accompanied by two guards. Since Lady Abigail's younger child, Damian, had tearfully begged his father to let Prudence come too, she also was allowed to attend. She held Damian's hand as they stood before the casket; Emanuel held the other.

Just before the interment, those attending were invited to throw flowers on the coffin before it was lowered into the ground. Prudence placed a single red rose; both Emanuel and Damian followed her example.

Then came the hollow thudding of the earth as it was shoveled onto the coffin, crushing, then obliterating the flowers that had been heaped on it. Damian stared at it, appalled. Prudence tried to draw him away from the grave, but he resisted. "I don't want to leave Mommy here alone," he said. "I want to keep her company."

"Your mommy's not here anymore, Damian. She's with the angels."

"You mean in Heaven?"

"Of course."

"Daddy doesn't believe in Heaven. He thinks that anyone who believes in Heaven is a fool."

"Daddy's not a happy man, is he?"

"I don't think so."

Prudence knelt in front of Damian and took both his hands. "Let me tell you *this,* dear: Your Mommy is way up there among the Angels. She sees everything you're doing, and loves you all the time. Every time you think of her, she keeps you company, and she helps you. Doesn't that make you feel better?"

Damian started to cry, and threw his arms around the kneeling Prudence.

"It's all right to cry, Damian; your Mommy knows you are sad. But she also knows that you won't be sad forever. And if you call on her, she'll keep you company when you are sad, and when you're happy."

"But is this true? Daddy says it's all a lie."

"It's not a lie, my dear. Thoughts like these come from God. So they *have* to be true."

One of the guards escorting Emanuel approached the Viscount, and said, "Now that it's over, we have to bring him back to the Compound, My Lord. But we just want to say that we're sorry for your loss."

Agright's lip curled. "Are you, then? Well, good for you." And he turned on his heel and stalked off.

NINE

We both need a break.

The Correction Compound (as Queen Anna liked to call it) was situated high on a bluff that overlooked a deep ravine. Arranged roughly in a semicircle with their backs to this ravine were fourteen dwellings built by recently treasonous nobles to house the eldest scions of their respective houses, to be held there as hostages to ensure the loyalty of the parents. Some of these dwellings were nothing more than cottages; others looked more like miniature mansions, such as the lordly edifice that Albemarle Agright, Viscount of Domeny, erected for *his* eldest son, Emanuel.

Count Edgar of Ravenshead, who had implemented the scheme, thought it unnecessary to build walls around the place, since it had more than adequate guards - four to each dwelling - constantly watching over it and over its inhabitants, who joked that it was impossible even to pee without the authorities taking notice. Any hostage witless enough to try escaping faced summary execution.

So it was well known to the authorities that there was a peasant girl, dressed in homespun, sitting near the precipice, enjoying the view and apparently drawing it.

"Who is your master?" a guard had asked. "What are you doing here?"

"I am a seamstress," the girl had replied, "and my mistress is Her Royal Highness, Princess Jane. She's given me the day off, so I thought I'd come here and draw."

"But the Castle Royal is a long way from here, it's quite a walk!"

She raised an eyebrow. "Take a look at that view – it's worth it."

In her bag they discovered articles both for sewing and drawing, and she did seem harmless. Yet there was something unusual about her: she spoke far more articulately than other young women of her class. So they decided to let her in, but monitor her carefully.

Thus, under their watchful eyes, the girl settled herself on a rock not far from the precipice's edge, produced her charcoal and her wooden slab, and began drawing. She quickly lost herself in her work, and was surprised to hear, "finding something interesting to draw?"

She quickly put down the charcoal and the slab, and gathering her plain-spun shawl about her, rose up to answer the tall young man. "My mistress says she won't need me today, My Lord, so I thought I'd take advantage of my freedom."

"Yes, by all means take advantage of freedom!" He smiled down at her.

She didn't blush or look down demurely, but steadfastly returned his gaze.

He nodded, smiling. "May I look at your drawing?" he said.

"Can I prevent you?"

"Yes, you could tell me not to. But since you haven't ..." Deftly he dropped to one knee to inspect her work. "Why, it's a portrait," he exclaimed, "and I know this fellow." He rose up as effortlessly as he had knelt down.

"Have you come here to draw him? You could have drawn as handsome a man anywhere."

"No, My Lord. I could only have drawn this *here* – nowhere else."

"I don't understand – why only here? Do you have some special connection to the man?"

"None whatever. But I want to draw the people who live here. I saw this man, once, before the revolt. I've heard that he's here now, but I haven't seen him yet; I'm drawing from memory. When I do see him again, I want to test if what I imagine is true – that a place can leave an imprint on a person who lives in it. I think I'd like to capture the imprint of the Compound on the faces here – where people are not free to say what they want, not free even to *think* what they want. That closes you down, I would imagine – having to be that careful."

"A profound little seamstress, are you – and talented, too! You're almost as good as Princess Jane."

"Oh really? How do you know?"

I've seen her work, though I've never had a chance to meet her."

"So I'm almost as good? I'll tell her that, next time I see her."

"You know her Royal Highness that well?"

"I do know her – though apparently not so well as I had thought."

"Why do you say that?"

"I haven't sorted it out, yet. When I do, I may tell you."

He looked at her speculatively. "Do you think she would approve of your visit here?"

"Her Royal Highness doesn't care where I go – so long as I show up for work on time."

“So it’s the Princess who is your mistress – and a liberal one, apparently! Then perhaps she wouldn’t mind your doing some sewing for *me*? – I mean when you have some time off from your duties to her?”

“I don’t know; I’ll ask her.”

“I pay well. Probably not so well as Her Royal Highness, but still maybe well enough ...” He left off, embarrassed.

“Well enough to entice me to sew for you?”

“Something like that.” His face colored, and he turned away.

Almost of its own volition, her hand began to reach out to him, but she quickly stilled it. “No need to be embarrassed, My Lord; I’m quite sure you pay well. I know who you are.”

“You do?”

“You’re Emanuel, eldest son and heir to the Viscount of Domeny, Albemarle Agright.”

“How do you know that?”

“Family resemblance.”

“You must have seen my father. Please don’t tell me I look like him.”

“Not at all. But you do look like your mother, poor lady, may God rest her soul. My condolences on your loss.”

Emanuel caught his breath, and was barely able to breathe, “Thank you.”

“It’s always difficult to lose a parent,” she said.

“Yes, especially when ... never mind.”

“I understand you, My Lord.”

He gave her wry look. “How can you understand how I feel ... I mean *really*?”

"I had the pleasure of knowing your mother."

He wiped his eyes, and took a moment to master himself.

"You did work for her?" he asked, finally.

"She owned some of my work. The Viscount has it now. Whether he chooses to keep it is another matter."

"If you produced work for me, I would keep it."

"You're very kind, My Lord."

"Well ... you could help me. Why don't you come soon ... I mean if the Princess will let you get away."

"I'll try to persuade her. But surely your father has left you plenty of servants for sewing and mending ... that sort of thing."

"But no one to talk to."

"And what happens if I should run out of conversation?"

"Then you can draw me. We'll see if you can capture the imprint of captivity on *my* face."

"That's too tempting a challenge to ignore."

"Possibly the Princess might want you to ignore it."

"Or she might encourage me to take notice," said the seamstress, smiling broadly. "I do believe she's becoming bored with me, and that we both need a break from each other."

TEN

I've met someone.

In the Castle Royal, the double, carved oaken doors accessing the Queen's apartment were always guarded by four soldiers handpicked by Lord John Flexner, who didn't like to take chances. One of the four greeted Jane: "Good morning, Your Royal Highness."

"Good morning, Henry. Is Her Majesty up?"

"Yes ma'am, and she gave specific orders not to allow anyone in without first checking with her. She's very busy."

Jane thought, *too busy to see her own sister?* But she said aloud, "Are there Ministers in there with her?"

"No Ma'am. Last time I saw, she was alone and working at her table."

"Could you tell her that I'm here to see her?"

"At once, ma'am," said Henry, who then knocked quietly on one of the doors, and on hearing an affirming voice within, opened it and went in, closing it behind him.

Jane tried to shrug off her irritation: *Of course Anna is busy. The weight of the realm is on her shoulders, and she's too conscientious to rely completely on all those long-winded advisors of hers; she knows all too well that the final responsibility is hers alone. What a burden – I wouldn't want it! So if she's too busy to see me I should be understanding and not add to her load by complaining. Still ... !*

Henry reappeared. "Her Majesty says to come right in," he said, whereupon the gloom of Jane's thoughts immediately lifted, and she went in to discover that Henry's description was accurate: Anna's table was piled high with sundry scrolls and parchments, from one of which Anna, a bit obscured by the load on her table, was taking notes with a quill pen. At the table's center, its crimson glow almost completely buried in the pile of documents, was the velvet-covered cherry wood casket, still enjoying pride of place in the room.

Without looking up, Anna, still writing, said, "Good morning Jane, just wait 'til I finish this thought ..." Jane felt a pang of guilt for interrupting, and she resolved to say nothing until Anna looked up. For a minute or two, the only sound in the room was the scratch of Anna's quill on the parchment. During that time, Jane noticed that in her eagerness to get to work, Anna seemed to have omitted certain fine details of her toilette. Her eyebrows for example, were not darkened, and her lips were not enhanced by color. *And yet look at her,* Jane thought, *she's still gorgeous. It's* not fair!

Finally, Anna replaced the pen in the inkwell and looked up. "Jane, dear – I'm so glad you're here. Please come sit down, next to me." Jane gladly complied. Anna continued, "I want always to have time for you, Jane: You're not only my sister, you're the heir to the realm in case something happens to me."

Possible replies were competing in Jane's mind: *Being your sister is more than enough. Why do you always have to drag in that heir-to-the-realm business? Do you think I've forgotten?* But instead of saying any of this, Jane smiled wanly.

"Now then Jane," said Anna the Queen, "what can I do for you?"

"You can listen to me."

"Of course, dear. What's on your mind?"

Jane shifted uneasily in her chair. "What I've wanted to say is ..." There was a long pause, a very long one.

"I'm all ears, Jane."

"What I've wanted to say is that ... I've met someone."

Anna said nothing, but simply gazed at Jane with widened eyes. There was a silence which Jane finally broke: "Are you dumbfounded, Anna? I haven't announced that I have the plague, for Heaven's sake; I've merely said that I've met someone."

Anna sighed, and took Jane's hands in hers. "You're old enough, Jane, and smart enough to know that a person of your station cannot choose for herself. Whom she marries is of vital concern to the state, to be deliberated and agreed on by all our ministers – even the ones you like to call long-winded."

Jane was quick to retort: "I remember that no such scruple entered your mind when you fell in love with Andrew Steele – at that time a lowly Colonel."

"Entirely different. You know very well that *then* there was a question of whether or not either of us would survive at all, let alone make matches advantageous to the state. I figured that if I had only a few weeks left to live, I might as well live them loving the man of my choice."

"This is so premature!" Jane cried. "I'm not saying I want to marry him – or anyone, for that matter. What I'm saying is that he interests me; more than anyone else I've ever seen *he interests me,* and I want to see where it leads – if anywhere – and I don't want to do it behind your back!"

"Thanks for that, at least."

Jane was breathing hard. "Give me some credit," she managed to say. "Do you think I would do anything to bring shame on us, or controversy? Your sister is better than that!"

"Of course you are, Jane dear," Anna said quickly, "I've never thought otherwise. And perhaps you are right; perhaps it is premature to get all excited about this. But may I ask, who is the lucky gentleman who has ... captured your interest?"

"He's captured nothing!"

"Piqued it, then. Who is this man?"

Jane pursed her lips, than blurted it out: "His name is Emanuel Agright."

"WHAT?! Of all the men in Grandlandia, you choose the son of our worst enemy?"

"His father *is* our worst enemy," Jane murmured, staring at the floor, "you're right about that. If wishes could kill, he would have slaughtered us long ago. I know that!"

"Why then ..."

Jane raised her head and gazed directly at her sister. "Emanuel is not like that."

Anna raised an eyebrow. "How long have you known him?"

"Less than an hour ... a few minutes, maybe. Why do you roll your eyes? How long did it take *you* to know that Andrew Steele was the one? You once told me that you loved him as soon as you saw him."

Anna the Queen rose up from her chair and walked a few steps toward a window. "You're the only one in this realm who dares bring up his name like that."

Jane got up, too. "Anna, for Heaven's sake, quit being the Queen for a few minutes, and just be Anna. I'm asking you: Do you think you are the only one in Grandlandia who can love at first sight?"

Anna turned to face Jane. "But how can you be so sure ..."

"I'm *not* sure, I tell you, but I want to find out! I know his father wants us dead. And I know that the apple doesn't fall far from the tree – except when it does. And I've reason to think that Emanuel doesn't like his father, may even blame him for his mother's death."

"Remarkable, the powers of intuition! You've learned a book full of knowledge about him from just a few minutes with him."

"Why are you surprised, Your Majesty? That's what *you* did. I learn from the best."

Anna seemed to lose a few inches in height, and sank wearily into her chair. "And how did you arrange this meeting?"

"I didn't arrange it. I borrowed one of my handmaid's garments – such as they were – and disguised myself as one of my servants, and told the guards that my mistress – the Princess – had given me a day off, so I took it to go drawing."

"And they bought it, did they?"

"They let me in. I went straight for a rock near the precipice and began drawing. I was so deeply into it that I didn't hear him come up behind me."

"Hear whom?"

"Emanuel."

"He could have thrown you into the ravine!"

"But he didn't. He was very polite. I told him the same story that I told the guards, and he seemed to buy it at first, but after a while, I began to wonder whether he wasn't seeing right through it. But he was too polite to contradict me, and acted as if he believed that I was the Princess' servant. He even asked me to beg the Princess to let .me come to him once a week – ostensibly to do his sewing – but really, he said, so he can have someone to talk to."

"And if you run out of conversation?"

"Exactly what I asked *him!"* exclaimed the Princess, excitedly, "and he said that should that happen – and let me tell you Anna, that won't happen any time soon – but if it should, he says, then I can try to draw him, and see if I can capture the impact on his face of being confined to the Compound."

"I see he knows just what to say to someone like you."

"Think what you like. I sense that he is a gentle, passionate soul – possibly just right for me."

There was a very long silence while Anna digested all this and Jane worried that she might have sprung too much on her sister too soon. Finally Anna said, "All right, Jane: You shall have your chance to find out. You shall visit him once a week, as he requests. No – don't thank me yet! First: Who is the servant whose clothes you borrowed?"

"Hannah Moro."

"Good! She is reliable and discreet, wouldn't you say?"

"She is the soul of loyalty and discretion," said Jane, "that's why I chose her."

"You did well. And on top of all that, she looks a bit like you. She has similar color, and has the same build – roughly."

"True, but I—"

"Don't interrupt," Anna said, "let me get this out while all the thoughts are still in my head. Here's what you'll do: Tell Hannah everything you have told me – *everything*. Then, once a week, you will wear clothes like hers, and the first time, she will dress like you and accompany you. I will designate a coachman to drive you both to the Compound, and another coachman to drive a coach full of soldiers to protect you just in case."

"But it's only five miles, and I'm perfectly able to—"

"I know you can, but that's not the point. Your walking five miles on a regular basis leaves you dreadfully exposed; it's too dangerous, and I won't put up with it. No – when the carriage arrives for the first time, it will contain you – pretending to be your own servant – and your servant, pretending to be you. And it will be accompanied by the second coach full of soldiers. Subsequently, there'll be only one coach, with only you as the servant. The security will be still there, but not visible. I'll ask Lord John to figure it out; he's good at this sort of thing."

Jane's jaw had dropped a little. "Why are you doing all this?" she whispered.

"The only way I could stop you," Anna replied, "would be to lock you up like a prisoner, and I won't do that to my sister. But I have other reasons, as well. If it turns out that the young man is not so gentle, or not so passionate, it will be good for you to have learned it sooner, rather than later. Right? And then too, you may learn something that would be good for your Queen to know before it is too late."

"You want me to spy for you?"

"That's an ugly word. I'd rather put it this way: You love me, and you love Grandlandia. You expect that he will love what you love. If he *doesn't,* you should know about it, and so should I. Is that fair?"

There was a pause, then Jane nodded.

"Good. And you shouldn't be surprised if at some point Emanuel hears the same sort of advice - or worse - from his father."

"He might. But to tell you the truth, Anna, I don't think he's the kind of man to follow the type of advice that Albemarle Agright might give. I just don't think he's cut from the same cloth."

"Well Jane, we'll find out, won't we?"

Jane's lips moved, but no sound was audible. Anna got up and moved to her, placing her hand on her shoulder and smiling down at her, almost maternally. "What was that, dear?" she said, "I didn't hear it."

Jane said, in little more than a whisper, "I'll find out."

Anna raised an eyebrow, so Jane added, a little more audibly, "I mean, we'll *both* find out."

ELEVEN

What a stupid idea!

"What a lovely evening this has been, Lord John," the Baroness Esther Hedley burbled, standing near the Lord's oak-beamed doors. "*So* many memories of color and light to take away with us!" She turned to her daughter. "Don't you agree, Angelica?"

Angelica blushed becomingly. "My Lord," she said, "I will treasure the memory of this evening forever."

General Lord John Flexner of Nightwood – the man-mountain, as he was called – wrinkled his face in puzzlement. "Forever?" he said, "You needn't go to all that trouble. But if you remember it until tomorrow or maybe a week at the most, wouldn't that be enough?"

The faces of mother and daughter fell, but Lady Prudence Alder, also standing nearby, rescued the situation. "Lord John is shy in these social situations. What he means to say is that he thought the evening simply lovely, truly one of the highlights of the season for him."

"Yes, yes," said General Flexner, "that's right; that *is* what I meant to say."

"Then perhaps," said Baroness Hedley, "we could invite the General to *our* humble dwelling."

Seeing the panic in Lord John's eyes, Lady Prudence once again sprang to his rescue: "If only Lord John were a completely free man, he'd welcome the invitation with all his heart. But right now, he is subject to the summons of Her Majesty to attend her at any moment of the day or night. For that reason, it may be a full year before he can hope to have another beautiful evening such as he enjoyed tonight. But he'll let you know."

"Oh please do, My Lord," the Baroness gushed. Then she turned to her daughter, and pronounced, "In the meantime, we must say good night to Lord John, mustn't we, Angelica?" Whereupon Angelica performed what her mother had taught her – a very deep curtsy, meant to show off her ample white bosom and its impressive décolletage.

Lord John bowed, smiling politely, and the smile stayed fixed on his face until the carriage containing the Baroness and her daughter was well out of sight. Then the smile faded as he slammed shut the massive doors himself, while the two servants whose duty this was stood by stiffly. "You can lock them now, if you like," he told them quietly, and stalked off into a large reception room, Lady Prudence following. When she was inside the room, she quietly closed the doors behind her.

"Well," said Lady Prudence, "how did you like the Baroness's daughter?"

"The same as all the others – for a brood mare she's very pretty. I could get lots of good-looking children on her – provided she could endure the pain of conception and survive the agony of childbirth. And even if she did, for the rest of my life, I'd be subjected to this: Oh, Lord John," he squeaked in a mincing, falsetto voice, "how honored I am to be in the same room with the savior of our country!" Then, in his real, rumbling voice, he said, almost shouting, "First of all, will people ever realize that I'm *not* the savior of Grandlandia, Her Majesty is! And second ... O Jesu! I'd gladly go through a day on the battlefield rather than have to endure another of these *social evenings!"* He started to pace back and forth in the room.

Priscilla didn't move, but followed him with her eyes. "I see that this evening's affair has left you in no better mood than any of the others."

He stopped pacing, looked at Lady Prudence, and said: "Look, dear: Maybe it's better to stop all this. Rather than trying to consign *myself* to Hell, why don't I just let Her Majesty do it *for* me and get it over with? Why should I fall on my own sword when I could receive the fatal stroke from Anna's own hand? Compared to more evenings like this, it would seem like a caress."

He sank down onto an upholstered bench and wrung his hands. "Don't further trouble yourself about me, Prudence, it's hopeless."

Prudence hadn't moved since she asked Lord John how he liked the Baroness's daughter, but now she made her way to the upholstered bench on which Lord John was sitting. "May I?" she asked.

He nodded almost imperceptibly, and she sat down next to him. "Lord John, I've never before heard you say the words, *it's hopeless.*"

"I've never felt that way before. I do now. I've been wasting your time."

"And so, you've abandoned all hope of easing your loneliness?"

"No – I'll get a dog."

Priscilla smiled wanly at him, shaking her head. "Dogs have limits. What you need is a human being who understands you. And if you're lucky enough to find her, you'd better bind her to you, share your life with her, and never let her go. There is nothing more precious. Don't give up. Keep trying, My Lord." Priscilla looked away, but not quickly enough to keep Lord John from seeing the tears in her eyes.

In Lord John's eyes, however, something was dawning. "You speak with great feeling, my Lady," he said.

"You don't know how lucky you are," she said, still looking away. "You're a man, and a supremely eligible one. Any unmarried young woman would be glad to have you. All you'd have to do is ask. But we women cannot ask. We have to wait for someone to ask *us*. And with every passing year, some of us know increasingly that we will never be asked."

"I'm sorry."

"Don't waste your pity on me. For freaks as tall as I – that's just the way things are; we get used to loneliness." She wiped her eyes and turned to look at him full in the face. "*But you don't have to.*"

This time it was Lord John who looked away. A long silence fell on them which ended when Lord John turned back to look at her, and saw that she was gazing at the floor. "Prudence," he said, "listen to me, I have an idea: Why don't *we* get married – *to each other?*"

"What a stupid idea!"

"No wait, listen: It's not so stupid. We both benefit. If, as you say, nobody else will ask you to marry, wouldn't that leave you waiting on the Queen for the rest of your life? Is that the life you want? But married to me, you'd have my entire staff waiting on *you*. You wouldn't have to lift a finger if you didn't want to. And I would treat you with the utmost respect. Separate beds. Separate bedrooms. We'd be man and wife *in name only*. But only *we* would know that. And you could go wherever you want, do whatever you want, without my say-so. You don't love me, do you?"

"What ...? I'm sorry ... what ...?" She was looking at him dazed, as if she hadn't really heard or comprehended much of anything he had said.

"I said ... I mean ... you don't love me, do you?"

"Oh! Well ... I scarcely know you – well I mean, I do know you a little but not nearly enough for ... anything like that ... anything *serious.*"

"*Exactly!* So of course, how *could* you love me? You don't, right?"

"No ... no, not really."

"Perfect! And as for me, I belong to Her Majesty. I can't imagine feeling that way about anyone else. So you don't have to worry about my starting to love you – it can't happen! Don't you see – this is perfect for both of us! I don't have to worry about Her Majesty foisting on me some empty-headed twit to whom I can't talk, and you don't have to worry about growing old as a spinster, still in service to royalty. You'll be freer than you've ever been, and I will be more ... I mean, really, *less* ... I will be less ... lonely. So how about it: Will you marry me?"

Lord John had the look of a teenager who had fallen in love with a bright idea.

Lady Prudence Alder finally found her voice. "You're proposing that we enter into a marriage of convenience, for the sake of appearances. You can continue being in love with the Queen, and I can be in love with whomever I want, go wherever I want, *do* whatever I want. We respect each other and agree never to violate each other's privacy – or anything else. We just put on a happily married front so – as far as the world is concerned – we seem to be the perfect couple. Is this it?"

"You've got it!"

"Well, I suppose we would not be the first, nor the last to enter upon such an empty show-marriage."

"Does that mean you agree? Is that a yes?"

Prudence gave him a faint smile, and said, after a long pause, "yes."

Whereupon the Man Mountain got down on one knee, reached for her hand, and kissed it. "Is this the right thing?" he asked. "I mean, I can do that, can't I?"

"Absolutely, My Lord," she said, her eyes shining.

TWELVE

Don't talk of death; talk of life.

By the time Anna the Queen met with her Security Council - Lord John Flexner of Nightwood, Count Edgar of Ravenshead, and Lord Turco of Pleasantvale – it was late in the morning. She had been sleepless half the night, and was fully awake well before the first morning light gilded the mountain-tops of Grandlandia. But even as the light began to warm the valleys, she lay quietly in bed lest her stirring waken Prudence, her Lady in Waiting. She felt strongly that her losing sleep because of worry about the country should not cause her countrymen also to lose sleep because of worry about *her.* And even though she was eager to discuss the state of the nation with her counselors, she delayed the meeting until what she felt was a reasonable time for them to accomplish their morning duties.

They arrived fresh and ready for business. If anybody noticed that the cherry wood casket had become a fixture in the room, none had the temerity to mention it. And Anna herself carried on as if it were not there. "Good morning, Gentlemen," she began, "I hope you all slept well?" Lord John and Count Edgar murmured that each had slept satisfactorily, and was grateful for her queenly concern.

But Turco had a different story. "Sorry to trouble everyone's morning," he said, but I just got word from one of my men that there is a mysterious spy-like activity going on. A stranger – nobody knows his name or where he comes from – has organized small parties of men to make maps of the countryside – showing roads, bridges, defenses and such."

Lord John roared, "this has been going on and only now you tell me?!"

"Calm yourself, My Lord. I just learned about it on my way over here. I've ordered my men to keep this stranger under surveillance and await further orders."

The man-mountain was about to erupt again, but then curiously subsided, with an odd smile spreading over his face. "You're not having one of your metaphysical moments again, are you, My Lord? Or maybe you're acting one of your roles – this time you're playing *super-spy*?"

Turco smiled patiently. "No my Lord, I'm not playing any role today. And as for my having a metaphysical moment, I fear the danger is all *too* physical. According to my information, at least one of their teams is at the Umbrian Canyon as we speak."

"Oh my God!" exclaimed Count Edgar, rising, "they couldn't have chosen a more dangerous place – with all its interconnecting caves and underground passageways – nobody I know understands the whole of it. By your leave, General, we should get at least three companies of light cavalry out there to surround the area very quickly, then detach a few score soldiers to see if we can sneak up on these spies."

"Would you take care of it for me, Edgar?" Lord John asked. "I'd very much appreciate it; I need to be in conference with Her Majesty."

"At once, General," said Count Edgar, who rose, then turned to his Queen. "With your permission, Your Majesty, I will withdraw."

"Permission granted, My Lord."

"Wait a minute," said Turco, also rising. "Shouldn't I come too, Lord Edgar? Don't you think you're more likely to find them with me?"

"We have to move fast. Can you sit a galloping horse?"

"Just watch me."

"We wish both of you gentlemen success," said Anna.

"Thanks Ma'am," they responded in chorus, and backed out of the room.

There was a silence, during which Anna the Queen and Lord John simply looked at each other.

"If you think you ought to go with them," Anna said, "we can postpone our conversation."

"It's not really necessary, ma'am. Edgar is experienced, and has good judgment, and he knows when to send word in for reinforcements if he needs them. I never have any qualms about delegating authority to him. And – to be perfectly honest – after Turco's revelation, I didn't feel good leaving you alone."

"Thanks," Anna said, "but what can you tell me? I'm sure that François is behind the map making."

"Without a doubt. Having maps is essential to any good military campaign – especially if you're unfamiliar with the territory." Flexner said.

"So there's no question that François intends to invade us?"

"None whatever. But if his romantic ploy succeeds, he'll save a lot of money and a lot of lives – French lives. Ours he doesn't give a damn about. His only motive is greed,"

"And to puff himself up," said Anna. "How I wish that his ship would capsize and drown him!"

"That's the right attitude for a Grandlandian Queen," said Lord John. "As for the Grandlandians making the maps, they're probably doing it to have something to eat. I think it's nothing personal against you, ma'am."

"I wish I could believe that," said Anna, but there are probably plenty of them who do have something against me. After we put down the revolt, I knew that there remained plenty of people who hated me still – mostly the nobility, who are all too willing to pass on their attitudes to the commoners around them. Which was why I came up with the idea of a Correction Compound. I was counseled against it. I was told it was better to put all my enemies to the sword – all of them and their families. But I couldn't do that. If I perpetrated that sort of violence, I'd have to spill even more blood to suppress the outrage that would follow. I'd be the Sovereign of blood, the Queen of death, Heaven forbid. I'd rather be dead myself."

"With respect, Ma'am: Your subjects love you, and would rather die than see you harmed. You have your whole life ahead of you. Don't talk of death; talk of life."

"Talk of life, should I? Is this your prescription? What are you, my physician?"

The man-mountain paused, then said: "I would be anything to you that you would allow me to be."

There was a brief silence, then Anna said, "I'm sure you would. But I've told you that I cannot let you love me the way you want to. Instead, I'll take your suggestion and talk of life. How's the wife search going? I'm talking of life, now. Do you have anything to report?"

"Yes, ma'am."

"And ... ?"

"Well as you know, I've been consulting with Lady Prudence Alder. She has been very helpful."

"I was sure she would be. And has there been any progress?"

"Yes ma'am. I have ... I have found someone to marry."

Anna the Queen leapt to her feet, causing Flexner also to rise. "Hallelujah! This is the best news I've had in months! And who is the lucky lady?"

"She is Lady Prudence herself."

Anna hooted. "Delightful! It appears that in helping you, Lady Prudence has been helping herself – and pretty freely, too! It's enough to make your head spin." She sat, and Lord John followed her.

"No ma'am, it's not like that. She was against it, strongly against it; she had other women in mind. But I didn't want them. Finally, I persuaded her."

"Wonderful! You have made me so happy, John. We will give you a state wedding!"

"With all due respect, Ma'am, we were thinking of a very small wedding, in the Chapel in the woods, with Friar Anselm."

"You shall have both. This is what Lord Andrew and I would have had – two weddings, a state wedding for obvious reasons, and a small ceremony because it would mean so much to *us*. You shall have what we would have had – everything you could desire, *everything*."

As he bowed, General Lord John Flexner of Nightwood did not say what he was thinking: *Not quite everything.* Instead he murmured, “Thank you, Ma’am.”

THIRTEEN

They always do.

"Whoa! What's going on?" cried Viscount Albemarle Agright, who had just been embraced vigorously by his son, Emanuel. "Why this sudden affection? Usually when I come to see you, you sit sullen in your house waiting for me to knock on your door. But now, all of a sudden, you run to meet me at the gate! What's happened?"

"I missed you, Papa," Emanuel said evenly. "Can't a man miss his own father?"

"Of course. But you've had plenty of opportunity to miss me before. Why start now?"

"I'm not starting. I'm just ... realizing how I've always felt. You shouldn't be so suspicious."

"Oh, I'm not, I'm not! It's just that ... hm." The Viscount subjected his son to a long, speculative look. "Maybe you're hiding something?" he asked.

"Like what?"

"Like the peasant seamstress who visited you. How'd you manage to get her up here?"

Emanuel experienced a brief flicker of anger, but quickly recovered. *Of course the guards would have told him; that was probably the first thing out of their mouths!* He smiled sadly. "I'm sorry to disappoint you again," he said, "but I didn't invite her. Her mistress gave her a day off, so she came up simply to ... look at the view. We just talked a little. She didn't even come into my house."

"Well, I hope you'll rectify that the next time."

"There may not *be* a next time," said Emanuel, "I have no idea of whether she'll come again."

"Oh she'll come again. I know her kind. Always seeking to better themselves with ... the right connection. You're probably not her first."

Emanuel stared at him, slack jawed. "Is that right?" he managed to say.

"Of course it's right," said the Viscount. "You think I don't know about these things? By the time I was your age, I'd already had plenty of experience with that sort of woman. Of course, I wanted all that stopped when I met your mother. And naturally, I didn't tell her about my romantic adventures, but I didn't have to. A woman expects that on her wedding night her groom will have learned about these matters *somewhere or other.* That's his *duty!* So if you want to invite a cute little seamstress up to your place, I'm delighted!"

"But I told you that I didn't invite her."

"Come on, boy, no need to hide it from me. There's no shame – quite the opposite!" The Viscount took the young man by the shoulders and beamed at him.

Emanuel removed his father's hands from his shoulders and turned away. "Apparently," he said, "It's getting easier and easier to please you."

The Viscount grew a little red in the face. "My boy, all I'm saying is that if you get the chance, invite the little chit into your house, have your way with her, and that will be perfectly fine! Enjoy yourself, and when you're no more in the mood, or when it's no longer appropriate, there'll be plenty of money to settle things with her family. They'll think it's a good deal; trust me, they always do."

The Queen of Life

FOURTEEN

Welcome to the home of the failure.

When Turco (then a Knight) learned that Anna his Queen intended to reward him with a Barony because of his priceless services to the crown during the recent uprising, he requested that the land grant be relatively small - no more than 100 acres. Others at Court sniffed at the modesty of this request, but Anna understood perfectly: This Master of Metaphysics had no use for outward ostentation, preferring instead enrichments of the soul. So Anna found 100 of the most felicitous acres in her realm - a pocket heaven with silver streams, green meadows, gentle rises, and rich woods - which Turco promptly named "Pleasantvale." And his lovely young bride Angelina, formerly a kitchen maid, cared not a whit that she'd be mistress of so small a domain. What mattered to her was that as Lady of Pleasantvale her Lord would be Turco, who was world enough for her.

And when they appeared at Court - very often in the first year - they seemed so lost in their mutual delight that everyone regarded them as "the lovebirds." But as the months went by, more and more frequently Turco appeared at Court social functions alone. When asked, "Where is Angelina?" he would reply, "Oh, she's home taking care of things," and most everyone seemed satisfied with that. But Prudence began to notice that no news of blessed arrivals was coming from Pleasantvale, so she wasn't completely surprised when one of Angelina's maid servants arrived at Court to tell her that

Lady Angelina would be obliged if Lady Prudence would honor her with a visit.

The style of the home Anna had built for Turco was very much like the home of his late mother (who died several months after their wedding). But instead of having merely two rooms they had ten, and instead of a thatched roof they had a roof of tile. When Prudence arrived, the door was opened by Angelina herself who exclaimed, "Lady Prudence, I'm so glad to see you!" and she curtsied before her.

"Dear, dear Lady Angelina, there's no need to curtsy before me."

"But you came so promptly!"

"I sensed you needed me. I'm not one to make a person wait if I can help it."

"Thank you so much! Do come in."

When they were in a small parlor, settled in chairs with a tea tray between them, they lifted their tea cups with conscious gravity, then took a long, simultaneous, ceremonious sip. Whereupon Angelina exclaimed, "why Lady Prudence, I see a ring on your finger – that's new, isn't it?"

"It *is* new – a gift from my fiancé."

"How beautiful! Who is the lucky man?"

"He made me promise I wouldn't reveal it until he felt the time was right."

"I hope the announcement comes soon! And the wedding soon after! And I wish you joy that lasts more than ..." Angelina pursed her lips, and placed her cup back in the tray.

"You broke off," Prudence said. "More than what? What were you going to say?"

There was a pause during which Angelina seemed to be choosing her words. "Lady Prudence," she said at last, "will you teach me to read? I know this is very sudden and you don't know me all that well and the last thing I want is to insult you, but I could pay you if you'd take the money – Lord Turco gives me an allowance and I'd be so glad to spend it this way – I mean, I'd work very hard, I'd try to be a very good student and you'd be proud of me and you could tell everyone you taught an ignorant kitchen maid to read!" The color had risen in Angelina's face, and she cut off as if she had run out of words and out of breath in the same instant.

Prudence became aware that her fingers were covering her mouth; she had reflexively raised them because her jaw had dropped. But she also became aware that Angelina was anxiously awaiting her answer. "Oh my dear Angelina," she said at last, it would be an honor to teach you. I am so moved that you asked; it must have been very hard to get up the courage to speak – am I right?"

Angelina nodded, wordlessly.

"Perhaps you'd been wondering quite a while if you dared ask me?"

"It's been months!" Angelina blurted.

"Months, you say?"

"Yes months since I guessed the truth ..."

"The truth?"

"That ..." and seemingly with great effort, Angelina spoke carefully: "the truth that Turco and I are *not* going to have the family we'd been planning ... You see, when we got married, that's all we could talk about – how many children we'd have, and what rooms they would sleep in, and how we would feed them, and what we would teach them ... And it was so lovely to be with him then, because I felt I was a worthy partner to him. Because - Heaven knows, there are so many things His Lordship can do that I can't, and I depend on him for all those things - I'm in awe of him, truly - but that's all right, I thought, because there's one thing above all else he needs *me* for - *to bear him children, and raise them.* And when it became clear that wasn't going to happen, I felt like a failure - useless to him!" Angelina turned away and got control of herself. Then she turned back to Prudence with a curious smile: "Welcome to the home of the failure."

Now it was Prudence's turn to speak carefully: "As to being a failure," she said, "nothing you've said so far tells me that you are necessarily the infertile one. It could be your husband."

"So what?" said Angelina. The result is the same - no children. "What can I do - be like Sarah in the Bible and offer him my handmaid Mathilde? You know - the one who brought you my message - pretty little thing, isn't she? All that blond hair - and dimples! I've been actually thinking of offering her to him, and wondering what I should hope for. If he failed to get her with child, then I'd be vin ... vin ..."

"Vindicated?"

"Yes, *that.* But the thing is, he'd be crushed to learn he was infertile. I wouldn't want to do that to him."

"Has Lord Turco ever talked to you about all this?"

"Never. He's the soul of courtesy. He insists that he loves me, and is proud of me - he doesn't say *anyway* but I'm sure he's thinking it - and he urges me to come with him to affairs at Court. But I just can't show my face there – I'm too embarrassed. And I keep thinking of offering him Mathilde. If he did get her with child, he would be so pleased, and maybe the child would be mine, in a way – and maybe the childbearing would loosen me up so I too could bear – I've heard of that happening. Still I might have to put up with Mathilde's secretly laughing at me just like Hagar, Sarah's handmaid, and I don't know if I could stand it! So I don't know what to do, except that if I learned to read, I could be there for My Lord in another way – I could try to keep him company in his thoughts. I could understand them, more. I could be a partner that way, at least."

Prudence took both hands of Angelina, and smiled deeply into her eyes. "My dear," she said, "you are doing the right thing. And I would love to begin today. But I didn't bring a book with me. Judging by your reference to Sarah and Hagar, I gather you're familiar with Bible tales?"

"I wish I knew more. But Friar Anselm has been teaching me about them."

"At St Barnabas – his Little Chapel in the Woods?"

"Actually no – he comes here and gives me private lessons."

"Such a dear old man!" said Prudence. "To come all this way ... he must like you."

"I don't know about that. But I'm *very* enthusiastic."

"I'm sure he doesn't encounter that too often," Prudence said. "A teacher will ride far to find an eager student. I suppose you have a Bible at home?"

"Of course! Turco wouldn't be without one. Shall I bring it to you?"

"Please."

Angelina sprang up and returned with a bible – a large ornate illuminated affair that had been part of Turco's family for generations. She opened it up and turned to a well worn page. "Look," she said, here is where they recorded the deaths, and here" she said, turning the pages, "these pages are for the births. There's room for some more – if only God would grant them to us."

"One thing at a time, My Lady. First, sit down by me so you can see what I'm reading."

So Angelina moved a chair next to Prudence, and sat down in it.

Prudence turned to the opening verses of the Bible and her finger traced the words as she read, *And God said, let there be light, and there was light.* "Isn't it wonderful," she said to Angelina, "that just by speaking, God could produce light where there was darkness before – *just by speaking.* Isn't it wonderful?"

"Oh, yes," Angelina breathed, "wonderful – and beautiful too."

"Yes it is beautiful, dear. And you too – just by speaking, speaking what you read – *you'll* be doing the same thing. You'll be creating light."

FIFTEEN

What are we going to do about Jane?

General John Flexner was having his daily consultation with Queen Anna in her large council room with its rough-hewn oak table surmounted by its cherry wood casket, when she was informed that Count Edgar and Lord Turco sought entrance. "Let them come in!" cried Anna, whereupon the door was opened to admit the two men. "Forgive our intrusion," said Count Edgar, "but we thought you'd like to learn what we found out at the Umbrian Canyon."

"Go ahead," said Anna, "what did you find?"

"A whole crew of peasants - some ten of them - who had been hired to map an area a bit to the North. Having done the work, they came back to the canyon to get paid - only to find that the man who hired them had disappeared."

"Any information on who this man is?" Anna asked.

"None, Your Majesty - except that they all agreed he had a foreign accent. A detachment of soldiers is bringing them in for questioning. Among them there's someone we're particularly interested in. It was he who made the map drawings and notations, so apparently he knows how to read and write. We'd like to learn what else - and *whom* else - he knows. Meanwhile, we've left the rest of our three cavalry companies to guard the area, with instructions to search the caves for the man who hired the mapping crew."

"I hoped you warned them about the dangers of that operation," said General Flexner.

"We did, General," Turco said. "We instructed them to send into the caves search parties of no fewer than three men, who should always keep in communication. We've left Lord Broadmoor – you know, Colonel Thomas Cryer – in charge of that operation."

"Good work, gentlemen; you have things well in hand," Flexner said. "Do keep me informed of any developments."

"We will General," came the reply – almost in unison – from Count Edgar and Lord Turco, who saluted and withdrew.

When they were gone, Queen Anna said, "this is obviously a matter of the highest consequence. If you feel you should go with them, you have our permission to withdraw now."

"I don't think I'm really needed," said Flexner. "My choices would have been the same as Count Edgar's."

"Well," said Anna, "we feel embarrassed to have to involve you in something seemingly trivial by comparison."

"Thank you, Majesty, but the way I see it, nothing you desire is trivial."

Anna the Queen heaved a deep sigh. "Your every action proclaims your devotion," she said, "so you need not always put it into words. Your deeds speak for you."

"Yes, Ma'am." *At least she notices,* he thought.

"And now, what are we going to do about Princess Jane?," Anna said. There's no way to prevent her from visiting Emanuel Agright, unless I lock her up – do you advise that?"

"Maybe that would be the safest, Ma'am."

"She'd never forgive me. I know how *I* was, when Lord Andrew was living. I know how I'd *be* if, by some miracle, he opened that door and walked in. No. We have to let her go."

"In spite of the risk?"

"With a Royal that age there's *always* a risk," said Anna. "It's your job to minimize it. What plans have you made to that end?"

"First thing, we've rotated out all the guards there and replaced them with twice their number. And they've been specially trained."

"Do they know that the visiting maidservant will be really the Princess herself?"

"No, ma'am." Sir John replied. "They've been told that the Princess has a special affection for this maidservant, hence all the precautions to protect her. And with careful preparation and with any luck, they will not recognize Her Royal Highness when she pretends to be Hannah Moro, and there's a good chance that Hannah Moro will get away with pretending to be Her Royal Highness."

"Excellent. What about the open door rule?"

"I stressed that repeatedly. If ever they allow the door to his room to close when she's in it, then that visit and all future visits will be cancelled."

"That's exactly what I told Jane," said Anna.

"Not only that, but I told them that if that door closes on them both, the whole company of guards will be demoted. Such is the Princess's solicitude for her maidservant's virtue."

"Perfect!" cried Anna the Queen. "I couldn't have done better if I had planned it all myself."

"Well Ma'am," said Lord John smilingly, "in fact you *did* plan much of it yourself – not that I mind, of course – it's always a special pleasure when you contribute to the planning. A very special pleasure."

"Yes, yes, John," said Anna, trying to keep the weariness out of her voice. "We know how you love us."

SIXTEEN

I think of you as the eye that sees.

The plan came off without a hitch. Hannah Moro, having been rehearsed how to behave like Jane, gave a perfect performance – at least it seemed so from a distance of thirty paces, which was as close to the guard house as Lord John allowed the carriage to come. From that distance, the guards saw the seeming Princess give the seeming handmaid a kiss on the cheek, a pat on the back, and a gay wave "goodbye." So they didn't look closely at Emanuel's youthful visitor, let alone interrogate her. But one of them did accompany her to Emanuel's ornate front door. Emanuel, having seen their approach, opened the door himself and heard the guard declare in a stentorian voice: "Her Royal Highness, Princess Jane, has sent you her handmaid to do such sewing as you may require."

"This is a signal honor," said Emanuel. "Would you please convey to Her Royal Highness my profound gratitude?"

"I can't right now, for my job is ..." and the guard took a breath, then delivered: "My job is to wait outside the door of whatever room the handmaid may be in, and make sure it is wide open. Failure to keep it wide open will result in the cancellation not only of this visit, but all others." The guard sighed in relief: This little speech, rehearsed so often that he said it in his sleep, was now out of him.

Emanuel turned to Jane. "Then wilt *thou* tell Her Royal Highness of my gratitude?" he asked, employing the second person singular used either with intimates, or, in a condescending way, with those of the lowest social class. The latter usage seemed more appropriate, here.

Jane nodded. “I will make sure she knows.”

“Then why don’t we proceed to the Solar,” said Emanuel, who led them to a large room used both as a bedroom and as a sitting room. As soon she heard where they were going, Jane was glad that the door was going to be wide open. When they got there, Emanuel said with a gesture, “get thee in there, wench; I’ll be with thee shortly.” Jane entered the room while Emanuel turned to the Guard. “Your job, I take it, is to make sure this door is open?”

“Yes, sir!”

“I’m grateful for your attention,” said Emanuel, who produced a coin and pressed it into the man’s hand.

“Oh no, sir, we’re not allowed to take tips,” the Guard said.

“Then give it to someone who needs it,” said Emanuel. And with that, he went into the room, and said to Jane, “let me get thee some sewing, so thou wilt not have come here for nothing. Art thou familiar with mending shirts?”

“Yes sir,” murmured Jane.

“Splendid. I’ll get thee a few.”

Emanuel went to the other end of the room to fetch them, while Jane produced a small sewing kit. It was ready as soon as he returned – which was in less than a minute. He placed them on Jane’s lap, and said, loudly enough for the guard to hear, “start with these, wench,” then added, almost in a whisper, “but why don’t we go to the other end of the room where he's less likely to hear us?"

They both got up and moved to a far corner which was well draped with tapestries. Near the corner was a table around which were four chairs; they each sat in one which faced away from the attentively guarded doorway. "Now then," Emanuel said very quietly, "if we keep our voices down, nobody will hear us."

"Thank you, sir," murmured Jane in a voice no louder than the undertone Emanuel was using.

As she began to sew, Emanuel said, continuing to use a low voice, "I'm sorry to have spoken to you so rudely. You are no wench, no commoner at all; you are most *un*common. In fact, until I saw you get out of that carriage with Her Royal Highness in it, I was convinced that you were she – Her Royal Highness – herself."

"And now what do you think?" she murmured.

"I don't know what to think. A moment ago I thought I saw Her Royal Highness kiss you goodbye. Which means – if I can believe my eyes – that you cannot be the Princess Jane. But neither can you be a handmaid – of that I'm quite sure. You are a lady, and I mean to treat you like one."

"But not where anyone can see us or hear us," whispered Jane, gazing steadfastly at her sewing. "Let my identity be my secret."

"Of course," he said. "Whatever your secrets, they are safe with me."

"As are yours with me," she said, catching his gaze quite frankly with her own.

"Then you've guessed I have secrets?"

Her smile mesmerized him. "Doesn't everyone?"

"I know I do," he said, looking shyly away. "I'm a secret even to my own father. He has no idea who I am. He would like to see me as a younger version of himself. But I'm nothing like him – not even close!"

"If I thought you were," she said, "I would not have returned."

"I'm so glad you did!" he blurted out.

"Hush!" she hissed. "If they hear us, then it's all over." She reached over to touch his hand. "Look: There'll be a time when we won't have to whisper. 'Til then, we must keep our secrets just between us."

There was a brief silence during which Emanuel looked away, deep in thought. Then he looked at her full in the face and said, "I have another secret to tell you. A few days ago, the guards told my father that a handmaid had visited me."

"Does your father know who I am?"

"How could he? The guards don't know, and I don't think *I* know. No – my father thinks you're some wench I've imported for ... matters other than sewing, if you know what I mean ..."

"I can imagine."

"Then maybe you can imagine how overjoyed he was, thinking that at last I was proving myself a man by taking advantage of some village maiden or other. My father is disappointed in me in that respect – in many respects, actually – but in that one most cruelly. I know he doesn't think I'm a real man. I'm not like *him*, that's for certain! Because what he did when he was my age was to leave a trail of broken hearts and bastard children all over the country. I'm sure my poor mother knew about them, but was afraid to say anything. My heart ached to see how miserable she was, and I vowed that I'd never prove my manhood the way he did. I won't have to." He lowered voice his even further and said, almost in a whisper, "I know my desire, and when the time comes, I won't do as he did; *I'll do it right."* Giving her a piercing look, he said: "I'll prove I'm a real man then."

"You've proved it now," she said, her voice quavering. "I feel I know you."

He took that in. Then he said, "But I don't feel I quite know *you.* Not that you should tell me your name – please don't do that. But all I know about you is that you are *she who draws.* I'm sure there's more to you than that, and I wish I knew what it was."

"I wish I knew too," she said. It would be lovely to be more than the hand that wields the charcoal."

"I think of you as the eye that sees."

"I know, and that's just the trouble," she said. "While others can immerse themselves deeply in the moment and enjoy it, I hang back and observe, so I can draw it."

"What's so bad about that?"

"I think it might be wonderful – every so often – to be so engaged in what's *happening,* to have so much *fun* that I *forget* to draw it."

Emanuel sat back and gave her a broad smile. "Well, we'll just have to work on that, won't we?"

"Absolutely," she said. "I look forward to it."

SEVENTEEN

Isn't it delicious?

Colonel Thomas Cryer was sitting in his double belled tent drafting a report when he was interrupted by a soldier running in, crying, "My Lord, My Lord!" There were blood stains all over the soldier's uniform, and he was obviously still bleeding.

"Mike! What's all this blood? Are you all right? Did you find him?"

"My Lord," came the breathless reply, "we didn't find him, *he* found *us!* We were in one of the smaller chambers - you could barely fit two men in there, let alone our party of three - when he appeared out of nowhere! A little guy, but he fights like a demon! Two of our men are down - both killed, I think, but I didn't stick around to make sure - figured I'd get back to you, while I still could. If he had killed the three of us, you might not have known what you were up against 'til it was too late."

"All right - you did the right thing. Get some attention for those wounds, soldier, and while you're at it, get Captain Thompson to find me five good men. We won't need you to lead us to the cavern. The blood you lost on the way out of there ought to lead us well enough."

When the soldier was gone, Cryer knelt and prayed to his Savior that he be granted a safe return home to see his beloved Mary and his two children, the younger being a little boy of only six months. Not that he expected anything especially life threatening to happen, although the little guy who fought like a demon might possibly be a challenge. Yet he was probably no match for Cryer, well known in the army for his skill with the sword. He wasn't afraid of the encounter; nevertheless kneeling in prayer before going into any potential danger had been his custom for years. Apparently it had served him well; others were following his example, and he wasn't about to stop now.

Before he and his detachment of five set off, he said to Captain Thompson: "If I'm not back in an hour, come in after me with a dozen men. Don't take any more. In those caves he can kill us off, one by one. So leave a good sized force up here. Maybe our encircling the caves has deprived him of food supply, which would mean he's growing desperate. He'll have to come out some time or other."

"My Lord," said Captain Thompson, "If all this is true, why go after him in the caves in the first place? There he can kill us off, one by one, as you say. Why not wait until he's forced to come out? Then he'll have to fight on our terms, and we won't have to fight on his."

"This is good counsel, Captain, and normally I would follow it. But I have a good feeling about this. He's only one man, and I never met a man I couldn't best with a sword."

So Cryer led his small group of five men down the hill towards the flats which contained the entrance to the caves. This entrance was in the side of the hill, a tall slit whose conformation led certain unsavory soldiers to refer to it with a coarse term relating to the female anatomy – a fact they made sure never to convey to Lord Broadmoor, who was notoriously straitlaced in these matters. Sure enough, the trail of blood led the men straight through this opening, and along a tortuous path where the chambers became smaller and smaller, their walls seeming to squeeze ever more tightly together.

They came to what might be described as a little foyer, which, to the right and to the left, had openings leading to other chambers. The trail of blood seemed to lead to the right side. "Hold up a second," said Cryer, whose voice, though quiet, reverberated through the cavern. "If this man wants to hide from us, he might avoid the right side, thinking we might try that first. On the other hand, if he were lying in wait for us, the right side is just where he'd wait."

At this moment they heard a disembodied voice: "Well reasoned, good sir, good thinking! I am indeed waiting for you in the chamber to your right – but don't move! There is room in here only for two to fight – three at the most. If you all come charging in here, I shall of course be forced to kill you all – just as I killed the unfortunate pair that entered here a few hours ago. Instead I have an offer for you."

"The only offer I will entertain," said Cryer, "is unconditional surrender."

"Oho!" came the voice, "very pretty, very pretty – but not very practical. Before you doom yourself and your comrades, why not hear my offer? I propose that you select one of your number to fight me alone – one on one. If I win – as I'm sure to – the rest of you can retreat unscathed. Or you can send in another to die, and another – until you gain wisdom."

"You're very sure of yourself, aren't you?" Cryer said.

"You've noticed that? But I'm also considerate, even thoughtful. The dead bodies remaining from the most recent fight have been moved into an inner chamber. Whoever comes in to fight me will find it rather dark in here. If the bodies had remained in the same chamber with me, my opponent might trip over them, giving me even more of an unfair advantage. So I moved them out of the way, to give my opponent a bit of hope – which for me makes it all the more enjoyable. And to entice you further, I will tell you that I am unarmed."

"What!"

"That's right. No sword, no dagger, nothing but ... little me. Isn't it delicious?"

"And you expect us to get rid of our weapons?"

"Oh, no, no, no, no, *no!* Bring in any weapon you want – or *all* of them if you like! I want to give you confidence – so the look of surprise as you die will be be all the lovelier for me. Yes, lovely – no other word to describe it. Using my skill to kill so many so easily – it's almost an ecstacy for me – even erotic, I dare say. It keeps me coming back for more! Now then: Choose my antagonist, so we can begin. Who wants to fight me?"

Cryer's five men immediately shot up their hands, but their leader said, "I cannot let this happen. You are all good men, to be sure, but I cannot let any one of you go in my place. I am the one he will face." He turned to the soldier bearing the torch. "You, Richard, stand by the chamber entrance. "He's used to this chamber and is probably counting on total darkness to give him an edge. Let's deny that to him, shall we?"

And so Thomas Cryer moved to the chamber's entrance, looked within, and saw, by the light of Richard's torch the small, slight man who had visited the Viscount of Domeny's mansion a short while ago. He was, as he promised, unarmed. The man spoke: "You, Richard, I'll thank to move that torch a bit forward so I can check your leader's hands." When Richard complied, the little man said, "My heavens, I see a wedding ring on your finger. And you've children at home?"

"Two, not that it's any of your business," said Cryer, almost spitting.

"Oh, but it *is* my business," said the little man. "It means I won't kill you. I'll merely maim you, so you'll see your family again – not that you'll be much use to them for a while."

Cryer had heard about all that he could take. "Shut up, you!" he cried as he lunged at the man, swinging his sword to decapitate him.

But the man deftly ducked, reaching up to seize Cryer's arm to pull him along the path of his deadly intention, causing him to slam into the chamber wall. The small man did not look back, but aimed at Richard a flying kick which punched his nose into his skull, killing him instantly. Beginning to fall, Richard let go of his torch, but the little man deftly caught it and tossed it back into the horrified group of four remaining men. "Don't stand too close to the chamber opening, my friends," he said quietly, "it's dangerous."

"*You* are a very dangerous man," Cryer said, still smarting from the collision. "Where did you learn to fight like that?"

"I travel a lot," said the man. "Are you ready for a couple more passes before I cripple you?"

Cryer circled around him, warily. He made a feint to the left, but the man did nothing to counter, as if he knew the promised blow wasn't coming. After two more such feints – one to the left, another to the right – Cryer lunged again, only to swing his blade at nothingness, while he felt a light tap on the side of his neck. Cryer felt as if he was in school again, and the man, like a patient teacher, was showing him that if he had put force into the touch, he could have broken Cryer's neck. But the Colonel cried out as if in pain, doubling up and falling to the floor.

The man walked over to where Cryer lay on the floor writhing. He peered down. "Were you hurt by that little touch? Did I get a pressure point or something?" Whereupon Cryer uncoiled, and with a huge effort swung the blade at the little man, who saw the blow coming – but not quite soon enough. A thin line of red appeared on the man's shirt right in front of his midriff. He grunted, and delivered a well aimed kick at Cryer's groin. This time the Colonel's groans were genuine. The man placed a foot on his ribcage, grabbed his wrist, and, with a twisting yank, dislocated his right shoulder. Cryer's face was ashen. The man looked down at the Colonel and addressed him soberly. "You played on me the oldest trick in the book, and I fell for it. Luckily, I leapt back in time; I got only a scratch. But what a humiliation! I was too cock-sure of myself – one of my character flaws. Let me tell you something, good sir: I'm not imprisoned in these caves; I can come and go as I like! Yet I have stayed here longer than I should, simply to have some fun – another character flaw, I'm quite sure. If you're up to saying anything, you can tell your men that I'm leaving tonight, but that they'll never see me. Oops – bragging again! When will I learn?"

Cryer emitted a piteous groan, and the little man knelt down, stroked Cryer's perspiring forehead, and said, "I could have killed you just now, my dear, but I promised I wouldn't. And I'm a man of my word – another character flaw, don't you think?

EIGHTEEN

Do you want to stay alive?

And so it was that close to midnight, Agright's Bull Mastiffs alerted the Viscount to the presence at the door of the very same small, slight man who had visited him not many days earlier. The aged Chamberlain Benedict led him – accompanied, as before, by four heavily armed guards – to the Viscount's study. But unlike the last time, the stranger seemed very much the worse for wear.

"What happened to *you?"* Agright exclaimed.

"A series of miscalculations on my part, Milord, the latest being that I underestimated how badly I had been wounded. I had thought it was merely a scratch – but as you see, not so. I need a place to hide and competent nursing to help me heal. You will of course provide both."

"I will *of course,* you say?"

"Please, Monsieur le Vicomte. Do you want to stay alive? Do you want your sons Emanuel and Damian to live? *Of course* you do, and so, *of course* you'll do everything I say."

Agright's response was terse: "Guards, kill him."

In the next five minutes, Agright was treated to a formidable display of the martial arts training that the stranger had acquired on his travels, doubtless on the silk routes to Asia. The stranger seemed everywhere at once, seeming even to fly through the air as he used the guards' weapons against them, their oafish, lumbering force no match for his agility, his focus. At the end, the guards lay dead, while the Viscount's study was a shambles. The Viscount sat open mouthed; his face white.

"Look what you made me do," said the stranger. "But I was merciful; I let you live. The next time, you won't be so lucky – and I won't spare your sons. No more miscalculations for me."

Agright managed to croak: "What do you want?"

"I've already told you what I want – shelter and nursing to help me recover. I need to get back my strength! What you just saw – I apologize for it; it's not my best work. Had I my full powers, killing those four louts would have taken half the time."

"But if I take you in, someone is sure to notice, which would mean the death sentence for my poor Emanuel."

"Very true, still *you'd* still be alive; so would Damian. But if you cross me, then it's death for the three of you, and I'll find help somewhere else."

Agright seemed to sag, as if the life were already seeping out of him. His answer was quiet and toneless: "All right," he murmured, "you win – whatever you want. May I call my Chamberlain?"

"Yes of course you may, My Lord; you need not ask permission: *You* are the master here."

So Agright rang his bronze bell – one of the only things in that study remaining in one piece – and soon Benedict arrived and surveyed the scene.

"Oh my God."

"Yes," said Agright. He indicated the stranger and said to Benedict, "this here is Sir ..." He paused and said to the stranger, "I'm afraid I still don't know your name."

"No names!" the stranger said forcefully. Agright tried again. "This here is Sir No Name. And *this* ..." he said with a broad gesture which took in the splintered wreck that was his study, and included the four corpses littering the floor, "*this* is his calling card. Sir No Name will be our guest for a while. Have a room prepared for him, please, and see to his every need. And after he's settled in, will you get some people to clean up this ... this ..."

"I understand, sir," said the faithful retainer.

NINETEEN

Better than nothing

Anna the Queen and Lady Prudence Alder were in the Council Room. Anna smiled at Prudence and said, "I've been waiting for you to reveal all the details of your engagement, but not one word from you. So tell me, what led up to it? How did he propose? How did you respond? I see he gave you a ring – did he give it to you when he proposed? Did he get on one knee? Did you cry? Come on now, tell me everything!"

Prudence smiled back. "Are you asking as my friend, or as my Queen?"

"That's a strange question," said Anna, a bit taken aback. "Why do you ask?"

"Well," said Prudence, "to my friend, I'd say only those things I was ready to say."

"You're saying that as your friend, I would not demand more than that."

"Yes, so please Your Majesty," said Prudence. "My situation as a bride-to-be is still so new, so ... unexpected ... that there's not a lot I'm ready to talk about."

"I understand. But can I ask you, at least, if you are happy?"

"Oh yes. Definitely. On balance, I think this is the right thing for both of us – for me and John. He thinks so, too. On balance. Definitely."

For a moment, Anna looked quizzically at Prudence. Then she took both of Prudence's hands in hers. "Dear Prudence, I understand completely. But, God willing, you both have many years ahead of you. And in time, things change. May God bless you both."

"Thank you ma'am." Prudence kissed Anna's hand, backed away from the Royal Presence, and left the room.

For a moment Anna sat completely still. Then she rose and went to the side of the table, where she reached for the velvet-covered casket. She removed the crimson covering, carefully folded it, and set it to the side. Then she opened the cherry wood lid, and very gently lifted out the slab of wood on which Andrew's portrait had been drawn. She gazed at it for a while, then said aloud, "I've been so busy, my love, I wasn't able to get to you today as early as I'd like. You know all about Prudence and John, don't you? My guess is that he proposed marriage lest I choose for him someone completely inappropriate. Of course I would never do such a thing, but probably he was afraid that I might, so he proposed. Poor Prudence. She knows the dear lamb doesn't love her; he probably *told* her so. Doubtless she has accepted him out of pity, and maybe – who knows? I know she respects him; she might even grow to love him a little. What kind of marriage can come from that? A better one than we have, my love. Hopefully they have some years ahead of them; while we – what do we have?

"I was furious when that Frenchman showed me your picture; I still am. If he thinks that an image of you – on this slab or on his face – can make me accept him, he's in for a painful surprise. I'd like nothing better than to kill him with my own hands. No – that's not true. Better than that – better than anything – would be to have you back again, my darling. If I could have you in my arms again, then nothing else would matter.

"How stupid it was of me to reject the last picture Jane drew of you. I thought I could never stand to look at it. But now – thanks to that hateful François – I have your image to look at every day. Most widows don't have so much; I'm very lucky. A picture of you is better than nothing."

Anna tried to blink the tears away, but failing that, placed the slab back in the casket lest her fingers, moistened by wiping her tears, smudge the drawing.

TWENTY

I am who I am.

Albemarle, Viscount of Domeny, looked tense. "I'm sorry I haven't been able to visit you these past few weeks," he said to his son, Emanuel, "but unfortunately I have been very busy with a business that I'd just as soon have avoided, if I could."

"That's new for you, Father. Normally, work comes first."

"It *has* been that way," he said quietly, "and I wish it hadn't." This was as close to an apology as the Viscount ever got. For him admission of error was a concession of weakness. But since he was closeted with Emanuel in his son's Solar – his combination bedroom and sitting room in the Compound – he felt he could safely say these things.

"What was the business you wanted to avoid – or shouldn't I ask?"

"Better not ask. It would be dangerous for you to know."

"Like that, is it?" said Emanuel, who got for an answer a few moments of silence.

Then the elder Agright said to his son, "But I hear that these past few weeks have been not at all unpleasant for *you*, my boy. In fact, you appear to have been having quite a good time."

"Just what have you heard?" Emanuel said evenly.

"That you've been visited once weekly by your so-called handmaid. Which by itself isn't that remarkable:

Lots of men in this Compound receive similar visits, and enjoy similar services."

"Watch it, Father: One more innuendo about her and this visit is over."

"What *is* remarkable," said the Viscount, continuing as if he hadn't heard the warning, "is the royal complicity in the whole affair. Your girl arrives in a state carriage, with the Princess herself accompanying on the second visit. It would appear that the Queen herself not only knows, but *approves* of these visits to you, of all people. And the open-door policy they have in place – that is truly remarkable. Do you know what I think?"

"I'm sure you're about to tell me."

"I think that this handmaid is no commoner."

"I'm sure she isn't," Emanuel said. "Her speech – her whole person – is too refined."

"I think I know her name," said the elder Agright.

"Then you know more than I do."

"You haven't asked her name?"

"I don't want to – not right now. When she's ready to tell me, she will – or she won't have to: I'll know it for certain."

"Do you know what, son: I have a contact among the soldiers assigned to guard this Compound. And he says that all his comrades suppose that your visitor is a commoner with some sort of royal indulgence. But I suspect that she is none other than the Princess herself."

Emanuel turned pale. "This contact of yours – have you told him of your suspicion?"

"No I haven't – not yet, anyway."

"If you do, then the visits will be over – and my life, too, so far as I'm concerned."

The elder Agright raised an eyebrow. "You've fallen in love with her! You have fallen in love with the sister of that ..." he lowered his voice to little more than a whisper "... that *bitch* who has meant nothing but evil to me and my whole family!"

"You have it all wrong, Father, said Emanuel, also in an undertone. "It is *you* who have meant nothing but evil to *her* since she became Queen. And all because you supposed that letting her live was a stain on your precious family honor."

"Watch it, son."

"Why? What are you going to do – disinherit me?" Emanuel's whisper was a hiss. "In a way you'd be doing me a favor. I could change my name, and nobody need know that I spring from the poison seed of Agright. You have conspired against the Queen and continue to threaten her crown. Any other ruler so threatened would have killed both you, and me, and Damian, and poor mother, if she were still alive. Instead, Her Majesty lets you live, and keeps me here."

Agright surprised his son by smiling. "Insolent, aren't you?"

"It's about time I was. When I ended up here, I had nothing to do but think. I thought of everything you did to Mother, everything you tried to do to the country. My days and nights were filled with hatred of you."

"Were they now?"

"But then *she* came, like a blessing from God. And I thought, if I weren't in this Compound, I might never have met her. And I thought, how ironic! The sweetest, the most beautiful days of my life I owe to ... the man who put me here. I have you to thank for *that too*, Father; I can never forget it."

The elder Agright stood silent.

His son continued: "I don't know if my visitor is the Princess or not. When she came the first time I suspected she was, but then when she arrived the second time and I thought I saw the Princess wishing her well, I didn't know what to think. And I decided it didn't matter. Then, as I grew to love her, I decided it *did* matter – a lot. For if she is indeed the Princess she is certainly not going to be allowed to marry a nobody."

"You're saying that a son of mine – is a nobody?"

"Compared to the Princes who'll be seeking her hand, yes – very much a nobody. But I can't worry about that now. In visiting me, she has given me a gift beyond measure. Whatever happens, I'll always be grateful for that."

There was a silence, ended at last when the Viscount said: "This young woman – does she return your feelings?"

"I hope she does. Maybe I'm flattering myself, but I *think* she does – which will do neither of us any good if she is Her Royal Highness."

"She *has* to be in love with you," said the elder Agright, "otherwise the Queen would never have gone to such elaborate measures to let her visit you, even incognito. Say what you want about the Queen – and I've certainly said plenty – she's not the type to jail her sister for loving the wrong man."

Emanuel flared. "Who says I'm the wrong man?!"

"Her whole council will, when they hear of it. Isn't it well known that I've often said – in public – that I'd ..." and here he lowered his voice to a virtual whisper "... that I'd *slit her throat* if I had the chance? And what I don't understand is why this ... this Anna – knowing all this – consents to Jane's seeing you *anyway*. What's the matter with her?"

"She's not like you, Father, but that doesn't make her sick. If she *were* like you ... well, that would be a different story."

"I just don't get it: in spite of everything I've done or tried to do, she lets Her Royal Highness see you anyway. *Why?*"

"To be honest, my guess is that – if indeed she is the Princess – she has told her sister that I am not like you."

The elder Agright once again smiled his curious smile. "Well, she'd be right about that. You're like your mother."

"And you're disappointed, right? You hate me for it, right?"

"No – on the contrary. In some ways, you remind me of her. I'm always happy to see you."

"You've a strange way of showing it."

"Well, showing affection has never been my strong point."

"Father, if you love me, please don't do anything that would ruin everything between me and the young woman. It probably has to end, anyway, but don't you be the one to cause it. I beg you!"

"And I tell you, my son, that it's too late to change me into a Christian Saint. I am who I am."

TWENTY-ONE

I was wrong about Her Majesty.

In the Highlands of Grandlandia stood an imposing fortification known as Fortress Steele, named after the late hero of the last war, a General still lamented by the nation. When Anna the Queen, still deeply in mourning for him, learned that Lord John Flexner of Nightwood intended to build the fortress in honor of Andrew Steele, she asked that he make it a grand monument to the hero, and Lord John agreed – so long as it would be not quite so grand as the Castle Royal, which was her residence. No building, he felt, should rival the Queen's residence.

Benedict, Agright's elderly Chamberlain, had rarely left the Viscount's mansion, and had never seen this new structure. When, at dusk, he beheld it for the first time, he got out of his carriage (he was too old to ride a horse), and gaped. Its massive crenellated parapets seemed like nothing so much as a giant dragon's teeth. For a moment he stood in awe, then, remembering his business, the old man, as forthrightly as his cane would allow him, walked through the front opening (the portcullis being up), and told his errand to the first soldier he could find, who promptly ran to General John Flexner with the news: "My Lord, there's an old man at the entrance who says he must see you, that it's a matter of life and death."

Benedict stood before the General holding a leather packet. "My Lord, my master, the Viscount Albemarle of Domeny, begs you read this immediately, and bids me wait until you have finished, that I may immediately follow whatever instructions you give me."

Flexner, who was sitting behind a crude table heaped with scrolls and parchments, stood up and took the packet from him. He opened the packet and pulled out a substantial sheaf of parchments, grunting at its size. "You are to wait, are you?" he said. "Well, you don't have to wait standing. Sit over there," he said, indicating a small bench, "so I may ask you questions as I'm reading this thing."

Flexner sat down with the message, squinted at the hasty scrawl, and began reading aloud: "My dear Lord John, by the time you read this I may be ..." And glancing at what lay ahead, Flexner decided to continue silently: *"... I may be dead, together with my sons. If my servant has arrived with this message, they haven't killed him yet, but they surely intend to, for he is the only one who can confirm in my story some details which you might otherwise disbelieve.*

"Three months ago, I was visited, late at night, by a stranger who looked to be about thirty. He said that he had arrived on the Bonhomme Marcel, and that if I would give him five pounds of silver, he would help me achieve what he said everyone knew was my deepest desire – to depose, indeed destroy Her Majesty. He said that if I did not cooperate now and in the future, he would see to it that my two sons were killed. I gave him the silver, fully realizing that it was treason.

"I asked him his name, but he refused to give it. 'All you need know,' he said, 'is that with those five pounds of silver, you are doing King François a great favor, and in

time you will find out that His Majesty knows how to thank people like you.'

"My Lord, I found out.

"As soon as he got the silver, he left, and presently I began hearing rumors of a large mapping operation, led, I presumed, by him. I also heard stories of a sizable army of soldiers sent out to arrest him, and smaller groups looking for him in the caves, only to be decimated by him. By him alone!

"He showed up at my place slightly wounded, and demanded I put him up and supply his every need, and threatened me and my children if I refused. Four guards were with me at the time, and I ordered them to kill him. But he – wounded as he was – killed them all. They were heavily armed and well trained, but they were no match for him. He was everywhere at once; he seemed to fly through the air! And the thing was: he was unarmed! All he used were his hands and his feet. My servant, if he's still alive, will verify this."

Flexner turned to Benedict. "Is all this true? Did he really fly through the air?" he demanded.

"I came in after it was all over," said the old man, "so I didn't see him do that. But the room was a shambles, blood and fragments of wood were all over the place, and the four men were dead. The little man had no weapons that I could see. And my master looked terrified. I've never seen him look like that."

"Very interesting. Let me go on reading this."

And Flexner continued silently reading: *"Not long ago he gave me a packet containing, he said, a bundle of maps. And he told me to bring them to a contact of his on the docks. His contact would know how to reward me. In private, I opened the bundle and saw that there were indeed maps, but in addition a little note that he did not tell me about. It told his contact that he was to kill the bringer of these maps. I include the maps, and the note together with this message to you.*

"My Lord, whether you succeed in killing me first, or whether that honor will go to my little guest and his confederates, I know I'm a dead man. But I beg you, save my sons! Emanuel is a good lad and is as different from me as day from night; he doesn't know a thing about my doings; he wouldn't harm a flea – please save him! He's still in the Compound where you put him. Save his life, and God will reward you! As for little Damian, he is just a child. I took him away and left him at the Castle Royal with Lady Prudence Alder, who is fond of him. Please show mercy, save him, too! As for Benedict, he has been loyal and faithful – although ignorant of my schemes – and doesn't deserve to die at the hands of Sir No Name – for so I have called him. As for me, I will not run away, but return home on the unlikely chance I can face down Sir No Name, as if that were possible.

"Before I die, I want to say that I was wrong about Her Majesty. I was too arrogant, too proud to see that she may be the best thing that has happened to this country in years, while I may have been among the worst, I'm afraid.

"I'll be at home. If you reach me first, I will surrender to you on the spot. But if, as I fear, Sir No Name strikes me before you can, I will fight him with all my might, and with the strength of the sixteen armed guards left to me. He may bring me down, but I won't go down without a fight."

Flexner placed the letter on the table, but kept his huge hand on it, as if the wind were blowing and he wanted to keep it from flying away. He had a lot of thinking to do, and he had to do it fast. If this "Sir No Name" was as dangerous as described, then Albemarle Agright, Viscount of Domeny might already be dead. He felt that at this moment, he had to be more concerned about the welfare of Her Majesty, in whose Castle Royal lived two of Sir No Name's prime targets – Damian and his temporary new guardian, Prudence. He must get Prudence and Damian out of there, then triple the guard assigned to the Castle, and put the place on high defense alert, which would include a security check of everyone living there, or visiting there. And it would do well to check the port to see who might be waiting there for Sir No Name's package of maps.

As for Emanuel, Flexner was not quite ready to trust the elder Agright's assurances about his older son's innocence. But he felt he had no choice but to protect him as well, for the sake of Her Royal Highness, if for no other reason. The truth would emerge later, but for now, Lord John could take no chances with Emanuel's safety. Where to put him, though? Indeed, where to put Prudence and Damian, to say nothing of Benedict? Why, right here at Fortress Steele, of course! Here there'd be plenty of soldiers, plenty of discipline. And above all, by the removal from the Castle Royal of the presumed targets of this Sir No-Name, Flexner would be lessening the danger to Her Majesty. He wanted this murderer nowhere *near* her. In Fortress Steele, the quarters, to be sure, were Spartan, and had been built with the supposition that only men would live there. So there might be privacy issues, not to mention issues of comfort. But his men would do their best to address these issues, and everyone would be reminded that these arrangements were *temporary,* until the current danger abated. And for the duration, *he himself* would live there to set an example as well as reinforce security.

Now what about secrecy? He remembered that on the eve of the uprising, elaborate efforts had been made to smuggle the females out of the castle by dressing them up as boys. But that was during the Coronation Banquet where so much was going on with such noise that nobody was likely to pay much attention. But this was a different story. There would be no way to disguise his spiriting away Prudence and the Agright children. People would see, and people would talk. Best to make no secret of the fact, but rather make it plain and public what was being done for security's sake. No need to go into detail about the reasons for the security; all would come out when it was fitting or unavoidable. Her Majesty, of course, would have to know the whole story, and as soon as possible. He'd send a dozen of his crack troops with orders to ride to the Castle Royal, deliver an explanatory letter to Her Majesty, then get Prudence and Damian, and bring them here. Another dozen of these elite forces with similar orders would go to the Compound to get Emanuel. This left – not including some twenty older soldiers – three dozen of these elite forces. One dozen would scour the port looking for anyone waiting for the cartographic package now in his possession, and the remaining two dozen would accompany him to Domeny, on the remote possibility that Agright might still be alive, or that Sir No Name might still be on the premises. It was worth a try. But one thing was sure: Her Royal Highness's weekly visits to Emanuel must *stop* for the duration. Now they were more than silly. They were dangerous.

These ruminations took no more than a minute to flash through Flexner's mind. Then he looked up at Benedict and said, "It was good of you to come; you did the right thing, and you'll be safe here. I'm getting Damian and Emanuel to come here, too, as well as Lady Prudence, for the same reason."

He rose and went into the large common room and started issuing orders. As each one was spoken, large groups of men suddenly quickened with activity. By the time he finished, the room was buzzing with purpose. He walked to a counter and swiftly wrote something which he handed to an aide. "Give this to Her Majesty," he said.

Then he walked to the stables, making his way to a stall whose walls were much taller and thicker than those holding the other horses. In this stall was Ares, a tan Destrier stallion. Destriers were known not only for their quick spirit, but also for their fierce temper. The fact that this Destrier was a stallion meant that these qualities were all the stronger in the animal. Besides Ares' trainer, the man-mountain was the only one who could ride him. "Good afternoon Ares," he said to the horse, which whinnied and shook with anticipation. "I'm glad to see you, too," said Flexner. "I'm sorry it has been two weeks since our last outing. But now we have a nice long ride ahead of us." He patted the animal. "We'll both enjoy that, won't we?"

TWENTY-TWO
Already At War

"My well-loved Queen," Anna read, "I regret to tell you that war with France may have arrived already. The spy we had heard about turns out to be a remorseless killer, a Frenchman in the service of King François. Having murdered some dozen of your subjects, he now appears intent on the death of Lord Albemarle of Domeny (who had once befriended him) and on the death of his two sons. As if it were on his death bed, Domeny has professed a complete change of heart, confessing that while he himself was one of the worst things ever to have happened to Grandlandia, you were one of the best. I've arranged to have Prudence, Damian, and Emanuel transferred to Fortress Steele, for their safety. For the duration, I will live there, too. Castle Royal will have its guard tripled.

"By the time you read this, Majesty, I will have left for Domeny to see if I can save the Viscount and apprehend the spy. I'll say more when I return."

Anna lifted her eyes from the letter and stared fixedly at a blank wall in her room, as if this castle wall were part of a prison, keeping her from seeing what was going on outside. If only she could see through that wall, she thought, and through all walls keeping her from knowing what Lord John was seeing at that moment!

If, by some miracle, Anna the Queen could have beheld what Lord John Flexner was seeing at that very moment, she might have regretted her wish. It was the Great Room in Viscount Agright's mansion turned into a charnel house, the humans in it turned into garbage, their remains scattered casually about like offal. The Viscount himself, in death, was offered no distinction or pride of place, being recognizable to Flexner only by an arm sticking out from a heap of cadavers, its wrist – crazily bent – still bearing the gold bracelet with the Viscount's vaunted family crest.

One of Flexner's subordinates – a young lad – turned green and vomited, which disgusted his comrades, who seemed indifferent to the carnage in the room. With a gesture, Flexner sent them out, and walked over to the lad, who was still retching.

"I'm sorry sir," the lad managed to say, "it won't happen again."

"Don't worry about it, said the man-mountain, patting him on the shoulder. "When I first saw death on a large scale, I wasn't much better. We all get used to it, I'm afraid to say."

"To things this bad?

"This bad and worse. Some times, the world can be a horrible place. So to spare ourselves, we let our sensibilities toughen up. We'd never get anything done if we let ourselves see just how awful the world can be, and how bad *we* have to be, sometimes, to accomplish anything in it."

TWENTY-THREE

You don't tell your husband that.

"And God saw everything that He had made, and behold, it was very good. And there was evening, and there was morning, the sixth day." These words were being read aloud by Lord Turco's young wife, Angelina, having begun reading lessons only a few weeks ago.

"Beautiful - perfect!" crowed Prudence, her teacher. "Your progress is amazing!"

"It's little enough," said the former kitchen maid, "when you think that all the cooking and cleaning are done *for* me, so that all I need do in the world is study."

"Well, not quite all," Prudence ventured. "I suppose that when Lord Turco comes home, some of your time is spoken for."

"You mean ... marital duties?" Angelina said with a blush rising in her cheeks. "Of course there's that, though not so much as when we were first married. Our desire for a family was all mixed in with our ... other desires, so that the joy of it all was sometimes almost ... overpowering. But when months went by with no sign of a baby coming, we got together less frequently, and our joy was perhaps ... not quite so much. And when His Lordship came home late from work, he never woke me up to love me as he used to do. He'd just slip into bed, and when I woke up there he was beside me - thank God! And I'd ask him why he didn't wake me up as he used to do, and he just said things like I seemed so lovely sleeping, and that he supposed I was tired, and in any case he didn't want to disturb me. The thing is, I *wanted* to be disturbed – very much! But I couldn't tell him that!"

"Why not?"

"Because ... you don't tell your husband that."

"You don't?"

"No! Because ... you want ... well *I* want ... to have him continue to think of me as his innocent angel, and to confess my desire would spoil it, somehow."

"It might not. Maybe you should try it."

"I couldn't. I'm not like that."

Before Prudence could reply, Angelina's handmaid Mathilde came running in. "Lady Prudence," she said anxiously, there are some soldiers – they look like Queen's Men – here to see you."

"To see *me* – truly?"

"Yes, my lady. They beg permission to come in and speak to you."

"Well," said Prudence, "if they beg permission to enter they're probably quite safe."

"Please show them in, Mathilde," Angelina said.

A few moments later Mathilde reappeared with a couple of young soldiers in tow. One of them said, "Lady Prudence, Lord Flexner has sent us to get you, and to bring you with us to Fortress Steele."

Prudence just stared at him, mouth agape.

"Oh!" the other soldier said, "we were to give you *this*." He handed Prudence a folded parchment – sealed, Prudence noticed, with Flexner's seal. She ripped it open, and read silently:

"My Lady Prudence – I have reason to believe that your life is in danger. The safest thing for you to do is to go with these men to Fortress Steele, where you'll have to live for

the time being. And I myself will be living there, too, to make sure you are safe and comfortable." For a signature, he scrawled something that looked a bit like a mountain range.

Prudence turned to the soldiers. "If you could go outside the house and wait for me there, I won't be but a few minutes."

"Please be as quick as possible, My Lady," said the first soldier. "We were told to hurry you along." And they both went out.

Rather than follow them immediately, Prudence showed the letter to Angelina, who exclaimed, "Danger?! Does this mean that Lord Turco and I are in danger, too?"

"I don't know. If you were in special danger, he'd ask you to come with me. Lord Flexner is *very* careful."

Angelina pointed to the mountain-range-like signature at the bottom. "What's that?"

"Oh that? It's simply M M."

"M M?"

"It means Man-Mountain. He says that he wouldn't mind my calling him that."

"So!" Angelina cried, "Your fiancé is Lord Flexner!"

Now it was Prudence's turn to blush. "Don't tell anyone."

Angelina smiled. "They'll never hear it from me," she said. "But may I ask you a question?"

"You can *ask.*"

"Do you ever call him Man-Mountain?"

"God, no! I don't dare. Not yet."

TWENTY-FOUR

I pity you. That's it.

When General Flexner strode into Anna's Council Room he saw that the meeting was already underway. Lord Turco and Count Edgar of Ravenshead were already there. "Terribly sorry to be late, Your Majesty; I came as soon as I could – been busy as a lodge of beavers."

Anna smiled. "We are not surprised, My Lord, and we've told your fellow councilors that you'd come as soon as you could."

"Thank you Ma'am. May I know the issue at hand?"

"This letter, My Lord," said Anna, handing him a piece of parchment. "Take your time with it; we'll need your advice on how to respond to it."

Silently, Flexner read: *"Most Puissant Majesty, it has come to our attention that our inveterate nuisance, Hector Vieuxtemps, has found his way to your realm and is causing trouble. He is practiced in the eastern martial arts, and, as you have doubtless learned, is extremely dangerous. He styles himself a close friend and agent of ours, and claims that we desire your violent overthrow. Neither could be further from the truth. Next month, we shall set forth toward your shores on a mission of love, and Hector Vieuxtemps is the ambassador we* least *need. We have arrested him twice, only to have him escape each time. He moves like quicksilver, and continues to elude capture. If your forces could apprehend him, or better yet, kill him, we would be deeply in your debt. Please do what you must to get rid of Vieuxtemps, so that when we finally set foot on your lovely land, no cloud will impede the sunny beams of love that will warm us both. Yours eagerly, François, Roi."*

Flexner snorted. "Sunny beams of love, eh? Humph!"

"Possibly it sounds better in French?" Turco offered.

"It's disgusting in any language," said Anna the Queen. "No sunny beams of love are going to shine on *us*. As for him, if the sunny beams of love should give him sunstroke on the way over, we would be mightily pleased."

"So say we all," said Count Edgar. But how do we respond?"

"It's very simple," said Flexner. "We tell him that anybody threatening Her Majesty – *anybody* – gets his eyes gouged out, his stomach cut open, and his guts ripped out to feed the dogs."

Anna smiled grimly, "Such a sight would not upset me in the least," she said.

"Nor me," said Turco. "The question is whether this language is ideal for our purpose, which is not to betray our awareness of his hostile intent."

"So what should we say?" Anna said.

"Tell him that we're grateful for his concern, and that we know how to treat enemies of the Crown. We wish him well, and say we look forward to his visit."

"Is anybody opposed to this language?" Anna asked.

Since no one indicated opposition to these words, Anna ordered that a letter be drafted incorporating them.

"It's hard to believe that Vieuxtemps is not really carrying out the will of his King," said Count Edgar.

"I agree with you," said Turco. "Which makes François all the more heinous, in my opinion. He gets Vieuxtemps to do his dirty work, then disowns him after he's delivered the goods. That his agent should be killed following his orders means nothing to François – Vieuxtemps is disposable."

"Are you then feeling sorry for him, My Lord?" Flexner said.

"Certainly not!" said Turco with noticeable irritation. "A spy knows the dangers of his profession, and fully deserves any punishment for crimes he has committed. And from what I hear, Vieuxtemps has done plenty."

"What is the outlook for catching this fellow?" Anna asked.

"Hard to say," Flexner said. "He's very smart, very wily. We have everyone on the lookout for him. He's dangerous, no question about it. But he's most dangerous when he's in enclosed spaces where only a few can get to him at a time. Out in the open where archers can get a shot at him, he doesn't present quite so serious a danger. The reason I was late is that I've been busy tripling the guard at Castle Royal, arranging for increased security scans of the place. I've taken the same measures for Fortress Steele, where not only will the late Viscount Agright's two children be staying for awhile, but also Lady Prudence. For some reason, Vieuxtemps has targeted the children, and since Lady Prudence is close to the younger one, I think it wise to take precautions with her as well."

Count Edgar cleared his throat. "Do you think we should be so interested in the children of an enemy of the Crown?"

"Before his death," said Flexner, "he seems to have had a change of heart, which we have reason to believe is genuine. The younger son, Damian, is just a child and presents no problem. As for the elder, Emanuel, I'm not quite so sure. But one thing I do know: It never hurts to keep your enemies close to you. If he is one, we'll find out soon enough."

"In that case, we have nothing more to talk about," Anna said. "Lord Turco and Count Edgar, your contributions are always most valuable, and we thank you for them. The same goes for General Flexner, but we have more business with him."

Having been thus dismissed, Ravenshead and Turco bowed and backed out of the room. When the door had closed behind them, Anna turned to Lord John. She got right to the point: "Lord John, this is a good time for you and Lady Prudence to be married."

The man-mountain stared at her, open-mouthed.

"No, I have not gone crazy," said Anna the Queen. "I can't think of a better time for it."

"With all due respect, Ma'am, I can't think of a worse. An invasion seems imminent, and with every passing day your life is in greater danger. There's a killer out there, and whether he's a loyal subject of François, a madman, or both, nobody is safe – you least of all. And just when I should be securing everything I can, you want me to take on the burden of a wife?"

"A burden would she be? Oh, please! I would say quite the reverse: She would make your burdens lighter – in all kinds of ways that women know how to do. She would be a help to you – not a burden."

"But this is the *wrong time,* ma'am!"

"It's the perfect time. The whole nation is apprehensive; they see our hurried war-like preparations, and they sense something is up. I want to show them that whatever is coming is not so grave as to postpone the spectacle and the joy of a State Wedding."

"A State ...? Your Majesty, it's just me and Lady Alder!"

"In case you have forgotten, Lord Flexner, you are the military hero of Grandlandia – that is, the surviving one. A nation needs its heroes to look up to."

"It has *you*, Your Majesty!"

"Yes, it has me. And if Lord Andrew had lived, it would have been *our* wedding that they would have celebrated, talked about for years. But he was too shy, and I knew that if it were to happen, I myself would have to make the first move. But I was too timid about it, and I kept putting it off – till it was too late for a wedding. John, with every fiber of my being I'm telling you: *Never put anything off!* I've learned my lesson – too late for me and Andrew, but not too late for you and Lady Alder. I cannot have my own wedding, but I can and will have yours, and I will invest it with everything my own would have had – if Andrew had lived."

"So I'm supposed to be driven to a wedding all the while an invasion is imminent and I'm worried sick about it?"

"Or you can exult that François has failed to prevent your marriage to your one true love – after all, it's your wedding you'll be driven to, not the scaffold."

"But this is impossible, Ma'am! Lady Alder is staying at Fort Steele – the safest place I could think of for her. She feels secure, and *private.* And of course, at night I am never so far from her room that I can't be there in a moment should she cry out."

"Very appropriate. What's the problem?"

"Well, there are hundreds of people working at the Fortress, working in it, protecting it. Day and night. There'd be hundreds of eyes on us all the time!"

Anna nodded. "Of course, I see your point: That would a drawback. But only a temporary one."

"But on our wedding night, all these people would be expecting us ..."

"What – to share the same room and go to bed together? I'm sure they *would.* What's wrong with that?"

There was a silence while the man-mountain, furiously blushing, stared at the floor.

Finally the silence was broken by Anna the Queen, who spoke very quietly: "I see you have no intention of consummating the marriage."

More silence.

"Does Prudence know about this?"

The word "yes" came from Flexner's throat, half choked.

"And she *agrees* to it?" The color was rising in Anna's face.

"Yes, my dread liege, she agrees to it! It's better for both of us. She gets all the support and protection that I can provide her, and also independence in life. She can go where she likes, do what she wants and she doesn't have to grow old in service ... to anyone."

"In service to me, you mean."

"I said to *anyone*, ma'am."

Anna rose abruptly, and Flexner rose with her, wondering if his legs would hold him. "I'd ask you what *you* get out of it," she said, "but I can guess." She started pacing the floor. "Your marriage will be a useful fiction. Not only will it shield Prudence from the buffets of the world, it will shield *you* from any unwanted marriage I'd command you to make – as if I could do a thing like that. Really! Did you think I would? Did you?"

More silence.

"Let me tell you something, My Lord: Had it not been for my devotion to Andrew's memory, I might have been in danger of falling in love with you myself. But after this last revelation from you, that danger is completely removed. It's gone. I could never love you – I pity you. That's it. As for your private life: it's none of my business. So go ahead – do what you want! But don't you dare harm Prudence, whom I love very much. You cause her to weep one tear, and I'll be on your back like an avenging fury! Do you hear me?"

Flexner stood frozen as she turned her back on him. He heard her heavy breathing, and scarcely dared breathe himself. Finally she turned back to him with a wan smile.

She spoke quietly and evenly. "But all this," she said, "is besides the point, which is that Grandlandia needs a State wedding, and I do, too. And on your wedding night if a hundred soldiers happen to press their ears to the wall, or their eyes to the cracks to see what's going on in your bedroom, I grant it could be a problem. But you're a resourceful man – I'm sure you'll solve it."

"I can't believe I'm hearing all this!"

"Believe it. Your wedding will be in six weeks. That will be all; get ready."

"Yes, Ma'am," murmured Lord Flexner, backing out from The Presence.

When he was gone, Anna the Queen walked to the center of the long table on which lay the velvet-draped casket containing the image of Lord Andrew's face. She reached over to it, placed her hand on it, and remained thus for some minutes, as if contact with the chest was giving her strength to go on.

TWENTY-FIVE

She'll know.

My dearest Emanuel," the letter began, "I just heard what happened to your father, and am aware of the inadequacy of words alone to comfort you. If only they would let me out of this pile of stones, this prison – that's what the Castle Royal seems to me now – I'd comfort you with more than words. But all I have is the Court's assurance that they'll bring this letter to you and bring back your response – if you should care to write one.

"You've told me that your father was disappointed in you, and it may have been that he was unsure how to relate to you, seeing that you were so different from him. But my guess is that when he lost your mother, he began to realize how deeply he loved you, as he saw her in you. He loved you, Emanuel, and he was proud of you, too – never forget that. I'm convinced that his last thoughts were of you and Damian.

"Much of his life was dark and full of anger, for which he paid bitterly. But he wasn't *all* anger. He loved your mother. He loved you and your brother. There surely was a vein of sweetness in him. That sweetness lives on in you, and I love it. You redeem him, my dearest one; you and your brother redeem him!"

"My heart is too full, and the circumstances too straitened for me to tell you all I feel. I pray God that the time will not be distant when I can be with you, and show you."

Emanuel pressed the parchment to his chest, and closed his eyes.

“Will there be a reply, My Lord?” someone asked, and Emanuel opened his eyes and was reminded that the messenger who handed him the letter was still waiting.

Inwardly, Emanuel thanked Heaven that he had had the presence of mind to bring with him a few pieces of parchment, a quill pen and some ink. “If you will wait outside,” he told the messenger, “I’ll write a brief reply.”

After the messenger was gone, he wrote: “Dearest Lady, waking and sleeping I see the way you have of smoothing your hair with your hand, the way you toss your head in joy; I see your gentle smile. You are always with me. Do with me what you will. I am yours for as long as I live.” Emanuel folded the parchment, melted some sealing wax onto the parchment and pressed his signet ring into it.

“Are you ready, My Lord?” the messenger called. “I must be getting back.”

“All ready, good sir.” The messenger entered the room and received the letter from Emanuel.

“Please put this into the hand of her who sent it.”

“I will, My Lord.”

“Not to anyone else.”

“No, My Lord.

“Tell her that I gave it you.”

“I will, My Lord. Anything else?

“Tell her that I ... no, don’t worry about it. If she reads the letter, she’ll know.”

TWENTY-SIX

You want to be whipped?

Sir Hubert Brookford looked up at the crescent moon peeping from behind the safety of dark, sullen clouds. He thought, *Not much light tonight! If they run to hide it's going to be much harder to find them. On the other hand, the darkness makes it easier to hide my horse, to say nothing of my back-up, thank God! If they saw the Queen's forces hiding in those trees behind me, they'd run like rabbits. With any luck, dressed as I am like a commoner, and arriving on foot, I'll seem to them no more than a domestic servant, on an errand for my master. May God have it so!*

Sir Hubert was in the port town of Middleburgh, through which a deep river ran to the sea. Grandlandia's few exporters found its location convenient, since it rendered unnecessary a long trek to the shore to ship their goods. It was here that Viscount Albemarle of Domeny was to rendezvous with the contact who would bring the packet of Vieuxtemps' maps to France. There were some half-dozen ships tied up alongside the wharves, but which of them held the contact in question? The ships themselves were totally dark, and Sir Hubert could see no one about.

"What's your business here, Sirrah?" said a man who had suddenly materialized out of the dark.

"I'm to meet someone who will receive a packet of maps that my master has given me."

"And who is your master?"

"More to the point, just who are *you?*"

"You question me, Sirrah? You want to be whipped?"

"My master instructed me not to give the packet to just anyone."

"I am not just anyone. I am Marcus Boatwright, and I oversee these wharves. And my master has been waiting for this packet."

"Could your master be, by any chance, King François of France?"

For a few seconds, Boatwright looked at Sir Hubert, the realization of his predicament beginning to dawn in his eyes. He began to run, but he was no match for the young knight, who caught up to him easily. Boatwright produced a small dagger, but instead of attacking Sir Hubert, he stabbed himself in the chest, grunted, and fell prostrate.

Sir Hubert knelt down by him. "You would die for King François?" he said.

"No," Boatwright gasped, "for my wife and children." Blood gushed from Boatwright's mouth, as he gurgled: "He said he'll kill them – *all* our families."

"*Whose* families?"

But Boatwright was dead.

TWENTY-SEVEN
What the truth is

I couldn't believe those words were coming out of her mouth; I thought maybe she was joking, or that maybe I'd wake up any minute. But no – she's dead serious, and this is all too real: Prudence, we're to marry in six weeks. Her Majesty has in mind a State Wedding such as they do for royalty – a real spectacle." Flexner was sitting on a crude wooden bench – the only thing in Prudence's little room that one could sit on, besides her bed. He was leaning forward, his head in his hands. Prudence sat next to him, a hand on his thigh.

"And naturally," Flexner went on, "after Her Majesty sees us safely married, and the public has cheered itself hoarse, you and will I retire for our wedding night in the only place safe for us both ..."

"Oh no," Prudence murmured.

"You got it – right here in Fortress Steele, with a couple hundred men listening, or *trying* to listen to every sound we make, and waiting to congratulate us when we finally emerge from our room."

Prudence removed her hand from his thigh. "What can I do to help?" she asked. "Shall I break off our engagement, say I've had second thoughts?"

After a very long silence, Flexner said "that's very sweet of you, Prudence."

"I want only what's best for you."

"I know that. But the thing is, it really wouldn't be best for me. Her Majesty would think I got you to do it, and she'd be even angrier with me than she is now."

"Why is she angry with you?"

"Because she knows ..."

"Knows what?"

Another silence.

"What does Her Majesty know, John Flexner? If you don't tell me, then our friendship will be as false as our marriage."

"Well that's just the point: she *knows* our marriage will be false."

"What – you told her?"

"No I didn't tell her!"

"Then how does she know?"

"Because the way the conversation went, what with me objecting to having our wedding night in the fortress, before an audience, as it were, of hundreds of soldiers ... and ... Her Majesty is a very bright woman, you know, and she suddenly said, 'you have no intention of consummating the marriage, do you?' and I said ..."

"Yes, John Flexner, what did you say?"

"I said nothing."

"You said nothing."

"That's right. And she asked, did you, Prudence, agree to it? And I said yes you agreed, because the arrangement was good for you: You'd have everything you wanted without having to work, and without having to grow old in service to anyone, but Her Majesty took offense at that—"

"I daresay she would!" Prudence cried.

"Anyway, Her Majesty became very cold to me, told me that if I made you cry even one tear, she'd be on my back like an avenging fury – those were her words. And she said she loved you very much."

"I'm glad *some*body does. Look John, you do what you want, and don't worry about my crying: I won't let one tear fall – I'm past all that." Prudence got up and went to the door. "Just leave me out of it. And when you've decided something, do me the courtesy of letting me know."

She opened the door, but Flexner sprang to his feet and put his hand on her arm. She shook it off, but he took her arm again. "Where are you going?" he demanded.

"What do you care?"

"I care a lot!"

"That's nice to hear."

"Well it's true."

"If it were true, you wouldn't have humiliated me in front of Her Majesty."

"You want me to *lie* to Her Majesty?"

"Does she have to know *everything?*"

"I've never lied to her. Do you want me to start lying to you?"

Prudence turned away from him, and murmured, "A nice lie every so often wouldn't be so bad. You could start by telling me that you cared for me."

"I just told you I did, and I wasn't lying. It was the truth."

Prudence turned back to him with a rueful smile. "Poor John. Do you even know what the truth is?"

"I used to think I did, but I'm not so sure anymore. All I know is that if you left me, I would feel more alone than I thought possible."

"I would feel alone as well, so don't worry, my man-mountain: I'll do whatever you want, even if it means marrying you."

TWENTY-EIGHT

We don't care what he thinks.

The preparations for the State Wedding proceeded apace. The plans were drawn up by Anna the Queen, who, from time to time, consulted with Prudence. On one occasion Anna asked her whether she liked the color blue.

"Of course, ma'am," she said. "Blue is a lovely color. But of course, the particular shade of blue can make a big difference."

"Well, this would be a dark shade – almost a royal blue."

"Oh?"

"Yes. It's for the carpet you will walk upon as you approach the altar. We can't have crimson, now, can we? That's what is used for royalty, and that would seem presumptuous – which I know is furthest from your nature."

"Thank you, ma'am. I would hate to step upon a crimson carpet, wherever it was."

"I know that, dear. So we'll settle on a carpet of royal blue, shall we?"

"Yes, if it please Your Majesty."

"*You* are the one it has to please – no one else."

"What about Lord John? May I ask if *he's* been consulted?"

"Unnecessary. If it pleases you, that's all he needs to know."

Prudence's face blanched. "Yes, ma'am," she murmured.

Anna reached out and took Prudence's hand. "Why, you're as cold as ice!" she said. "Look, Prudence, our love for you hasn't diminished; if anything, it's warmer than ever. But as for Lord John Flexner of Nightwood, other than matters of state security, we don't care what he thinks."

That seemed to be all too true. When Anna's council of advisors met, she no longer asked Lord John to remain for a private conference after the council's business was finished. When she dismissed her councilors, Lord John bowed out with the rest of them.

Not that she wasn't acutely attentive when he spoke of his continuing search for Hector Vieuxtemps. Intense and exhaustive interrogations of everyone known to have seen him had yielded nothing. And among the populace, the spies planted everywhere on Her Majesty's service had reported nothing odd, no rumors of anything unusual. All the same, he said on the first of these tense meetings that the forthcoming state nuptials - Anna had just announced them - deserved the highest security possible, including sharp-shooters on the roofs, soldiers dressed in plain clothes scattered among the crowds of on-lookers, and keen-eyed captains dressed as postilions astride the white horses drawing the wedding carriage.

"I seem to remember something similar on my coronation day – the day I married the state," Anna said. "My beloved Andrew came up with almost the same thing."

"Your Majesty, I tried to make it *exactly* the same thing. I was there and I paid attention. It *will* be the same – except of course that Prudence will be in her own bridal carriage, not with you, and ..." His voice trailed off.

"And Andrew will be nowhere," said Anna, tonelessly. "You don't need to remind me."

TWENTY-NINE

How To Save Your Marriage

Once out of the council room, Lord John tried his best to get away as quickly as possible. But since Anna had chosen that meeting to announce his forthcoming nuptials, Flexner had to make his way through the congratulations of his colleagues. Count Edgar of Ravenshead, as always, was generous with compliments and good wishes. "What a lucky woman Lady Prudence is, and what a lucky man *you* are to get her! May you both have every good fortune!" Lord John Flexner allowed himself a taut smile, and submitted to Edgar's enthusiastic embrace.

"Thanks so much," he said, "I'll tell Prudence of your good wishes. In fact, I'm supposed to be seeing her now, and I'm a bit late, so I really have to go. But thanks again!" And with that, the General of the Queen's Forces started off briskly.

"Wait! Wait up," cried Lord Turco, running after him, "let me congratulate you, too!"

"Flexner turned around and faced Turco with the same taut smile. "Oh, sorry My Lord," he said, "I was in a hurry and didn't see you."

Turco was a bit out of breath, and tried to keep from panting as he managed, "Angelina would never forgive me if I neglected to extend to you both our warmest congratulations and good wishes."

"Thank you, My Lord, that's very kind of you and Lady Angelina. But now, if you'll forgive me—"

“Just one more thing, General, if you don’t mind – some personal advice?”

“On how to save the country? Haven’t you given me enough of that for a while?”

”No, General, it’s not how to save the country. It’s how to save your marriage.”

“This sounds interesting,” Count Edgar said. “May I come closer, so I won’t miss anything? Margaret and I are still doing very well, thank God, but they say you never can tell.”

Lord John shrugged his shoulders, and the Count drew closer.

“It’s inevitable,” Turco said, “that some days you might feel frustrated or disappointed, or you might wonder what got you into the marriage. That’s the time for you to remember why you fell in love with her in the first place – that’s the secret. You simply focus on what you saw in her when you were drawn to her. Concentrate on that and things will feel better. It always works.”

Count Edgar spoke up: “May we take it that from time to time, Lord Turco, you yourself practice this ... secret?”

“I’m not ashamed to admit it. And when I focus on the lovely qualities that drew me to Angelina in the first place, invariably I conclude that my disappointment is caused by a lack in myself, never in my darling.”

“This is great advice, My Lord, and it’s worth bearing in mind – isn’t it, Lord John?”

“Oh, yes of course,” said Flexner, “well worth bearing in mind.” But inwardly he wondered how the advice could apply to him. His forthcoming marriage to Lady Prudence, as he perceived it, was not so much caused by his attraction to her as it was caused by his fear of what would happen if he did *not* marry her.

THIRTY

I will do no more playacting.

Normally, when Angelina practiced her reading, she tried to put the bible away well before Turco got home. But this time he arrived earlier, in full daylight – mid-afternoon – and she was so absorbed that she didn't hear him as he came in and saw her sitting on a bench with the bible in her lap.

"Hello!" he said, "looking at the bible, are you? Interesting!" He sat down next to her on the bench and kissed her.

"Actually I'm doing more than looking at it," she said, smiling at him. "I am trying to read it, My Lord."

"Truly!"

"Yes. Shall I read something to you?"

"Oh, yes, please – I'd love that."

So Angelina pointed to the first word in Genesis, and then, as she pointed to each word, recited slowly: "In the beginning, God created the Heaven and the Earth."

"That's beautiful!" Turco breathed. "But how did you ...?" Turco's face furrowed.

"Lady Prudence is teaching me how to read."

"What – did she volunteer to teach you?"

"No. I asked her if she would, and she said yes; she was very kind."

"Good for you both – wonderful! But what brought this on?"

Angelina looked away from him, and gesturing to the bible, said: "Somewhere in here it says that Sarah offered her maid Hagar to Abraham, in the hope that Hagar might bear upon Sarah's knees and strengthen her."

Turco – usually never at a loss for words – stared at her dumbfounded. "Darling, what on earth are you talking about?"

"Sarah felt bad," Angelina continued, "because having a son was so important to Abraham, and she was unable to bear him any children at all."

The light began to dawn on Turco. "And you feel the same as Sarah, is that it? I've told you, Angelina, that you are not necessarily the infertile one. *I* may be the one. Whatever. The way I see it, this may be the portion that God has allotted us, and I will not – *cannot* – love you any the less because of it, and I hope you feel the same way."

She fought for control and managed to say, "I do, more than I can tell you." Then, in a voice which she hoped sounded restrained, she continued, "which is why I thought I might offer you ..." She broke off.

"Offer me what?"

Speechless, she gestured toward the bible.

Turco thought a moment, and then his jaw dropped. "What – you would offer me Mathilde? That's the most—"

"Wait," she interrupted, "listen to me: She loves me and she said she'd do it for my sake ..."

"You actually *asked* her?"

"... Please listen: she's very pretty and might bear you a beautiful son who'd carry on your wonderful mind and who knows, it might quicken me so I too could bear and be of some use to you!" At this point, Angelina could hold back no longer, and she burst into sobs.

"Oh, my poor darling," Turco said. "Let's put that book away, shall we?" And he rose, closed the bible and put it in its place of honor in their small parlor. Then he returned to her. "Angie, I don't want to hear any more about Mathilde. She's no lovelier than you, but even if she were, you're the only one I want. We can always adopt, if it comes to that."

"But what about—"

He stopped her question with a kiss. "No more, darling." He sat next to her. "Do you want to tell me about your reading?"

She put her hand up to her throat. "What should I tell you?"

"Well, how far along have you read?"

"I'm at where God makes Eve out of Adam's rib."

"Ahh," he breathed, "one of my favorite stories."

"Mine, too. And ..." She paused, as if considering whether to go on, then continued: "Do you think it's interesting that Eve was once part of Adam just as light and darkness were once all mixed up together, so God creates them by separating them out? Do you think that's interesting?"

His eyes widened as if he were seeing her for the first time. "I *do* think it's interesting, and I think *you're* ... just wonderful! To think all that is in that pretty head of yours – the combination's very alluring."

"Oh!" she cried, her face coloring.

"But let's explore the metaphor. Do you think it means that I was once part of you and you part of me?"

"I often think so, and I wonder if that's why we ..." She hesitated.

"Long for each other?" he prompted.

"Yes. So we can feel complete? Is that it?"

"It is with me," he said, "I feel that way right now – *very* incomplete." And with that he picked her up in his arms and carried her into the bedroom. Her fingers were just as eager to disrobe him as his were to strip off her clothing; her mouth was just as avid for kisses.

She gasped when he entered her with one long, slow thrust, and she gazed into his eyes intently as she said in a low, guttural voice, "my love, did you enjoy our bible conversation?"

"I loved it," he said. "To hear you speak that way excited me tremendously," whereupon her eyes closed and she had an orgasm – her first ever.

After a few more such climaxes – Lady Pleasantvale was proving to be the mistress of more sensuality than either of them had suspected – she lay in Turco's arms, her shuddering stilled, and her breathing slow and deep. "Darling," she said, "you're really *you,* aren't you, and not someone else?"

"What a strange question! Of course I'm me – who else would I be?"

"Well, during the rebellion, to help Her Majesty you'd often pretend to be someone else. Sometimes you pretended to be a spy for the rebels; sometimes you pretended to be a cousin that didn't exist ... I lost track of how many disguises you created. You were really good at it, and I admired it, but it was also a little scary, and it makes me think, *when he's with me, is it really* he *who's with me, or someone else pretending to be Turco? Or maybe it's really Turco, all right, but he's only pretending to be here with me – his mind is somewhere else.* Darling, I don't want to make love with anyone else but you – really you; I want *all* of you, when you're all there with me, and not pretending you're there when you're mind is somewhere else."

He started planting little feather kisses on her forehead. "Demanding little thing ... aren't you?" he managed to say, between kisses.

"Well, we each have a right to ask it of the other, don't you agree?"

"Oh I agree with all my heart," he said. "In fact, before we married, I vowed to myself that there would be no playacting in our marriage, and I tell you right now: I will do no more playacting *outside* the marriage either – unless of course, Her Majesty requires it of me."

Having unburdened himself with these promises, Turco was about to prepare himself for slumber when he noticed that Angelina was not yet sleeping. "Is there anything on still your mind, dear? I notice you're still awake. Are you worried about anything?"

Angelina opened her eyes. "No – nothing's worrying me. I just was wondering if I could say how beautiful it is when you come home early."

"I feel the same way. That's why I *come* home early, when I can. Seeing you sooner is better than later."

"I just want to say that I never would have believed how beautiful, how exciting it can be when we get together. But it's even more wonderful *when we do it in the daylight*, because then we can *see* each other as we love. That is a precious gift for me – for us both, I hope."

"Of course, darling, for me, too. I may not always be able to bring us this gift in the short days of winter. But in the summertime, I hope to bring it to us every day."

She sighed, and kissed him.

He was preparing more reassuring words when he noticed she was fast asleep.

THIRTY-ONE

Have I abdicated?

When Lord John Flexner entered the royal conference room and knelt before Anna, his reception was chilly.

"I see you no longer care to be punctual," said Anna, his Queen, looking at the ceiling and sighing as if in great ennui. "You're more than two hours late."

"Forgive me, Your Majesty. "Someone tried to kill me."

Anna snapped to full attention, and stood up, and he rose, too. "Are you all right?"

"Yes, thank God. The assassin was a rotten shot with a crossbow – missed me by a mile. The whole thing was strange. After shooting the bolt at me, he put down the crossbow, took a flask out of his pocket, drank from it, and then just lay down. So I rode up to the shooter and asked him did he want to die – attacking me like that – and – can you believe it – he said yes! He said he was a farmer, not a fighter, and had shot at me because a mysterious man had given him the crossbow and a flask of hemlock poison, saying that if either I or the shooter weren't dead by the end of today, the mysterious man would kill the shooter's wife and kids. I asked him who this guy was, but the dying man said that his family would be killed if he gave out any information that would help locate the fiend behind all this. I wanted to ask him more questions, but he stopped breathing. So I slung his body over my horse, and rode with it back to Fortress Steele. No man there recognized him. I told the men there to bury him. He's not the first to die because of

Vieuxtemps – the one behind it all, I'm quite sure – nor, I fear, will he be the last."

There was an aching silence, broken by Anna: "That poor man."

"That poor man indeed," said Flexner, "to say nothing of his poor wife and children."

After a pause, Anna said, "And our poor country – terrorized by a monster nobody seems able to catch."

"We are doing the best we can, Ma'am, and we might be able to do better if so much of our energy weren't taken up by providing security for this ... wedding."

Lord John would have said "*accursed* wedding" if he had dared – a fact that did not escape Anna the Queen. "So now," she said, "you would like me to cancel the wedding."

"No, not cancel it," he said, "but postpone it for a week or two – a month at the most, till we can find this bugger – forgive me, ma'am – and send him to hell where he belongs!"

"You know as well as I do, John, that very likely in two weeks King François will be here to darken our realm. And when that happens, we will need all our resources, all our faculties, and can have no distractions, *then!* If we are to have the wedding, we must have it before he arrives."

"But *why* must we have this wedding, Your Majesty? Nobody around here seems to want it except you."

She gave him a wan smile. "Isn't that sufficient, My Lord, or am I no longer sovereign here? Have I abdicated in favor of Hector Vieuxtemps? Why aren't you making obeisance to *him?*"

Flexner was staring at the floor with a look so abject that Anna softened her tone.

"Come," she said, "let's sit down at the table." They did, and Anna put her hand on Sir John's. "I know you would never dream of bowing to anyone other than me. You're our most loyal servant. But you are wrong about one thing: I am not the only one desiring this wedding."

"Who besides you?"

"Why Prudence, of course."

"Forgive me, Ma'am, but when we last spoke, Lady Prudence was furious with me. The last thing she wants is to marry me."

"Strong words. What might have brought on this fury?"

Clearly embarrassed, Flexner didn't answer right away. But Anna prodded gently. "I asked you," she said quietly, "why was she so furious?"

"She said I humiliated her," he said at last, "by telling you everything."

"Of course! Telling her everything you revealed to me certainly *would* embarrass her; I don't blame her for feeling humiliated."

Anna briefly considered giving Lord John a lesson in the tactful handling of the gentler sex, but quickly abandoned the idea. Whereas Andrew Steele had been adept both on the battlefield and in the courts of love, such flexibility was too much to expect from General Flexner. "Look, John," she said at last, the thing for you to remember is that Lady Prudence loves you deeply."

"Impossible! How do you know?"

"I'm a woman; I know. And I also know this: When someone is lucky enough to find a person who loves them that way, he or she must bind that person to them with hoops of steel. There is nothing finer in life."

THIRTY-TWO

May God protect you.

My dearest Emanuel," the letter began. "Tomorrow is the wedding day for General Lord John Flexner and Lady Prudence. Her Majesty sets great store in this match, and wants to celebrate it as if it were the state wedding that she would have had if General Steele had lived. Much of her resources are being thrown into the festivities; it will be a Very Significant Event indeed! Naturally, she wants me to attend and to have the honor of riding in the Royal Carriage with her. Lady Prudence was to ride in her own Bridal Carriage, but at the last moment the plans were changed to have her ride in the Royal Carriage with us. Apparently it's a bit safer: The Royal Carriage is sheathed in steel armor, and they claim that it is (somewhat) more resistant to crossbow bolts than is the bridal carriage – though I fail to see how safe it can be with all those window openings provided to let the people see us.

"Luckily in Fortress Steele you will be as safe as it's possible to be in this perilous realm (I've heard the rumors about Hector Vieuxtemps), but I will have to take my chances along with everyone else in the Royal Carriage. This sort of thing never bothered me before; it comes with being who I am, and I have accepted it. But lately I've been thinking that I'm no longer living just for myself, I'm living also for you, dearest one. I want to be there for you as long as I can, and it's tormenting me that I am not with you *right now.* We both must pray God not only to let us live, but to let us live *together.*

We live in perilous times, my love, so dangerous that we are forced to consider what lovers don't want even to imagine, that we can be parted by some *force majeure* beyond our power to control. And of course it's true: Sooner or later death must part us. It could happen, hopefully, after many, many years of a loving marriage – may God so will it! But it could also happen *tomorrow* – which makes me think that whether it happens sooner or whether it happens later, *the price of love is pain.*

Should fear of that pain constrain our love? *I say no!* Rather let the certainty of eventual loss – may it not happen for years and years – make our love all the sweeter and more poignant. And so may it be with us, my darling.

I never used to set much store in prayer, but now that so much is at stake, and I am so powerless to do anything about it, I do a lot of praying!

"In my prayers I also include Lord John and Lady Prudence, as well. He's been so devoted to Her Majesty that I never thought he'd look at another woman, let alone marry her! And I wonder if these nuptials may have been more than a little influenced – even instigated – by Her Majesty herself! But Lord John is the rock of stability, and once he sets his mind on something, he'll doubtless do everything in his power to see it through. Prudence too is steady and firm of purpose, and in height she's as much a match for the man - mountain as is any female I've ever seen. Each of them deserves happiness, and I pray that this marriage will be enough to secure it for them.

"Meanwhile, dearest, set my love as a seal upon your heart. I am for you alone – always."

The reply came swiftly. “My darling lady,” it said, “I must be brief because our messenger tells me he must return immediately. I echo your expressions of love and courage, and can add only that I long for the day when it will be *my* arms defending you. May God bless you and protect you tomorrow.”

THIRTY-THREE

Be adult about all this!

"Now what?" said Lord John Flexner after he and his bride, Lady Prudence, had entered their private quarters in Fortress Steele, and had closed the door behind them.

Prudence raised her fingers to her lips. "Shh," she whispered, "as the bridegroom of the hour, you're supposed to *know* what comes next. Don't let the listeners know you have any doubts on the matter."

"Of course I know what's *supposed* to happen," Flexner said, *sotto voce,* "and I have no doubts of what *is going to* happen. You are going be in the bed, and I am going to sleep on the floor."

"Whatever you wish, My Lord. But there's no need to do this immediately. If you like, we can talk for a while. I don't mind if the listeners hear us."

"Won't they think that a long conversation means a lack of desire on my part?" Flexner whispered

"More likely, they'll suppose it means a maidenly shyness on mine - which ..." (and here she drew very close and whispered very low, her lips brushing against his ear), "*if this were real, it certainly would be.*"

She sat down on the edge of the bed, and he raised his hand to his ear, which was still tingling from her lips having brushed against it. "Then," he said, "if a conversation is normal in this situation, why not? But do we still need to whisper?"

"No, My Lord. Talking quietly will do."

"Well then," he said, "what did you think of the drive to the cathedral?"

"You can sit down, My Lord – next to me if you like." She patted the edge of the bed next to her, and he sat where she indicated. "Now then," she continued, "you were saying ...?"

"I was saying that was some drive to the cathedral – what with the crossbow attack and all. I wish I had been available to chase after those bastards."

"I'm glad you were not," she said. "One doesn't have to be a great shot to hit the man-mountain. Anyone who can hit the side of a barn door could have hit you, My Lord."

"Possibly – although it might not have hurt me much if I'd been wearing my proof steel armor – which is what your carriage had. They told me those bolts never punched through the carriage's steel, thank God."

"When they hit," she said, "you could see the wood break and the steel punch in – maybe a half inch or so – but the steel never broke. We all pressed ourselves as far back as possible in the carriage to present a lesser target to those shooting through the windows."

"Good thinking!" cried the man-mountain.

"It was Her Majesty's command – although I for one was already doing it even before she said it."

"So Her Majesty was very cool about this, was she?"

"She seemed so. She barely raised her voice when she said, "Press yourselves back – although right after that she did shout, 'Drive on faster, *faster!*'"

"That last was unnecessary – those were standing orders."

"I thought so. She had scarcely started shouting when the carriage picked up speed. We had to hang on for dear life, the jouncing was so hard!"

"You must have been terrified, My Lady."

"I wasn't exactly thrilled," Prudence said evenly, "but I thought, if I can survive this adventure in one piece, I'll get to be married to Lord John. I'll become Lady Nightwood, though maybe I'll allow my close friends to call me *Mistress Man-Mountain.* So it all will have been worthwhile, don't you think?" Prudence gazed steadfastly at the earthen floor.

There was a moment of silence which Prudence broke again by looking directly at Lord John, and repeating, "don't you think?"

"I'm terribly sorry, Lady Prudence."

"Don't mention it; I'm a big girl."

There was another silence, which Prudence broke again. "All through the reception," she said, "all through the interminable speeches and the drunken toasts, I couldn't get my mind off of those four crossbowmen. I had been told that by the time they were found they were all dead – from suicide, it appeared."

"That's right. Apparently they were terrified that Vieuxtemps would kill everyone they loved."

"What sort of man could use his power so cruelly? I'm terrified of him, too."

"Prudence, I'll try my hardest to protect you."

"How can you? Her Majesty comes first."

"That's true for everyone in the country. If something happens to Her Majesty, then nobody is safe. Her Majesty *has* to come first. But within that, I'll do my best to protect you. I *want* to because—"

"Don't say it," Prudence interrupted. "I don't need any lies, especially from you."

"It's not a lie, and I *will* say it."

"Please don't."

"I must! I'll do my best for you because you're my ... special friend."

There was a pause during which she just looked at him. "I know I am, John," she said finally, "and I feel the same way."

"You do?"

"At the very least," she said, favoring him with a wry smile.

They gazed into each other's eyes, and then he looked away. "I suppose it's now time for us to go to bed," he said. I'll step outside while you prepare for bed. When you're in the bed, call for me, and I'll come in and take the floor."

It didn't take much time for Prudence to prepare for bed, and when she called for him, John came in, snuffed out the light, and was about to lie down on the floor when Prudence said, "I'm cold, John."

"I got the warmest blanket I could find."

"It's not enough. I'm used to more. Come lie in the bed next to me; I need the warmth."

"But I don't think—"

"*Don't* think. Come to bed; I won't bother you, but I refuse to allow you to sleep on the floor like a dog."

"You refuse to allow?!"

Prudence spoke very quietly, "do you want me to start screaming? Just get into the bed and warm it up. Do it now."

So Lord John Flexner, wondering whether her imperious command was a foretaste of the new marriage, took off his clothes and got into bed. He was relieved to learn that Prudence had shifted to the other side of his great bed so that he would not touch her inadvertently, and he began to relax. Then a thought occurred to him: "What will they think when they see that there's no blood on the bedding?" he said.

"Don't worry, there will be blood."

He started to get tense again. "And just how will we manage that?"

"It has already been managed. I brought a bit of goat's blood in a leather bottell and smeared it in the bed before I got into it. The chambermaids changing the bedding will see that you deflowered me dutifully."

This woman thinks of everything, he thought. "Thank you," he murmured.

"You're welcome."

"And the listeners may just as well go to sleep now," he said a little more loudly, "as there'll be nothing more to listen to."

"Oh, is it noise you want?" said Prudence, who then, in a very loud voice put on a performance: "Oh! Oh! Ohhh Ahhh! Aieeeee! *Aieeeeeeeee!*"

And muffled, as if from a distant room, came the sound of cheers and applause.

"Oh my God," Flexner groaned. "Did you have to do that?"

"I thought you wanted it. I want to be a good wife to you, My Lord, and supply whatever you want. Now everyone should be happy."

"Are *you* happy?"

"Hm-mm-mm," she murmured contentedly, "now I can sleep." And before long, her deep breathing told him that she was indeed in the first stages of light slumber.

As he lay there, he became aware of the fragrance she had put on before lying down. And to make matters worse, Prudence, now more deeply asleep, had turned on her side and was snuggling closer - apparently to get warm. *This woman is distracting!* he thought. *How will I sleep?* To distract himself from the distraction of her, Flexner rehearsed in his mind how he would deal with the flotilla of French ships that he was sure was gathering just over the horizon. *For all I know,* he thought, *they could be here tomorrow morning! Well, let them come - that'll keep me busy, and I won't have to think about her.* But Prudence, now even more deeply asleep, had placed her hand on his arm. His eyes opened wide as he stared into the dark. *I'll just take her hand off me and put it ... where? No, no - regardless of where, it would be churlish of me to remove her hand. But she would never know! So what? I would know. And what if, in her sleep, she put her hand on me again? Am I to stay awake all night so I can remove her hand each time she puts it on me? Ridiculous! Get used to it, Flexner. Besides, it's only temporary. When this emergency is finally over and the danger has abated, we'll live at my manor house, and will have separate bedrooms. Easy solution. So it's only a matter of time. Be patient, Flexner, she's really a very nice lady and she cares for you. Things could be worse. Be adult about all this!*

And so, busily planning how he was going to be adult about all this, Lord John Flexner distracted himself from the distraction of her in the bed beside him, and was oblivious to the danger that was in fact now gathering just over the horizon.

THIRTY-FOUR

Then she saw him.

When the door knock came shortly after sunrise, both General Lord Flexner and Lady Prudence were wakened from sleep.

"Sorry to wake you, My Lord," came the voice from the other side of the door, "but we've spotted ships a half mile from shore!"

"How many? No wait ... let me get my clothes on." And Flexner bounded from bed and threw himself into his clothes, uncaring that his lady's widening eyes were filling with the sight of him. *Have I married all that?* she thought. But she had the presence of mind to draw the blanket up to her chin so that when Flexner opened the door a few moments later, the messenger – Sir Hubert Brookford – would have beheld a reasonably decorous scene, had he cared to look in. But Sir Hubert did not care to look in. He too had presence of mind, so that when Flexner opened the door, he saw that Sir Hubert was politely looking away from it. Lord John, however, turned back to the doorway and said "Sorry my dear, but this is urgent business. I'll have your chamber maid attend you."

"Be careful, my love," said Lady Prudence.

"I'll do my best," said her husband, closing the door. He turned to Sir Hubert. "Now then: How many ships were there?"

"Three. One was a bireme, which looked to have on each side two rows of rowers, each with thirty oars; the other two had on each side a single row of twenty oars."

"Where were they heading?"

"They weren't moving. Their oars were mainly still in the water – except for an occasional stroke or two to maintain their position, which was parallel to the shore, according to the lookout. He said that they seemed very well trained."

"Parallel to the shore, were they?" General Flexner asked. "From your description, they must *want* to be observed, and are waiting for our response. Very likely, the bireme contains King François and his attendant lords; the other two have the rest of his entourage."

"What are your orders, My Lord?"

"Get a longboat – not too large, about eight oars to a side – and get it ready on the shore opposite the French ships. I'll meet you there with sixteen oarsmen. Run!"

"Yes sir!" said Sir Hubert, who took off speedily.

Lord John went to his office and dashed off a brief note, then went to the Common Room, found a courier, and said, "put this note into the hand of Her Majesty."

"Your Majesty," she read, "it appears that François of France may indeed be about to set foot on our realm – *today!* I am redoubling security for the Castle Royal, and am preparing a military escort for him and his entourage as he makes his way to you. When he disembarks at Middleburgh I will have a chance to see this fellow in the flesh. You will get *your* chance in a few hours."

"Your Majesty!" said the courier, "are you all right?"

Anna, the crumpled note still gripped in her hand, had turned pale, and had begun to waver unsteadily on her feet.

"Help her Majesty!" the courier cried as he ran to steady her.

Within seconds of hearing this, members of her court were rushing to their Queen, who already had recovered enough to say, more loudly than was necessary, "I'm fine, I'm fine!" The courier quickly released her and stepped back, but Anna, still a bit shaky, went to him, gripped his hands in both of hers, steadying herself further. She said, very quietly, "you see I'm fine; thank you so very much. Let one of my courtiers know your name and where you live, that you may know a Queen's gratitude."

"No, please, ma'am. Just being able to help you is all the reward I could hope for. Please continue to feel better." And with that, the courier bowed his way out of the Presence.

Anna straightened and said to her courtiers, "find out who that young man is. I want to reward him somehow."

When Sir Hubert Brookford's sixteen-rower longboat led the three French ships into the port of Middleburgh, they found fifteen carriages, a dozen mounted knights, and five hundred foot-soldiers waiting to welcome them. The Grandlandians were keenly interested not only in the bireme (none of their ships having more than one file of rowers to a side), but they were also curious to see whether that large ship would fit into its slip (it did – just barely). The other two ships fit easily, as of course did the sixteen-man galley.

The first Frenchman to disembark was not King François, but one of his courtiers, soon followed by another. These two worthies flanked the exit ramp extending their hands to offer assistance in case His Majesty would need their help getting out, but François brusquely waved their hands away. His courtiers backed off from him, allowing him to become the sole focus of all eyes as he stepped onto the dock at the same moment the sun came from behind a cloud, shining brilliantly on his crimson and purple raiment, and giving the impression that today, the sun had decided to shine for His Majesty alone. Clearly savoring the moment, François smiled broadly.

General Flexner, clad in proof steel, walked toward him. *Remarkable!* Flexner thought, *this man could easily be taken for Andrew Steele -- the cut of his beard, his bright blue eyes, his carriage – it's almost spooky.* But as he approached him he thought, *Ah, look: When you get closer you can tell the difference: General Steele was lean and muscular, but* this *fellow – not so much. Steele's features were chiseled, but this fellow's face – it's a bit on the fleshy side, I would say. Still, the similarities are striking! But will they be striking enough so that someone* looking *to* _*find*_ *resemblances – someone maybe like Her Majesty – can persuade herself that this is Andrew Steele* to the life?

By this time, Lord John stood before François. He bowed, and said, "Your Majesty, I am General John Flexner, Baron of Nightwood. Her Majesty Anna, Queen of Grandlandia, bids me welcome you and express her hope that your visit will be pleasant."

Whereupon King François, in perfect Grandlandian, replied, "I thank *you*, My Lord, and I look forward to thanking Her Majesty *en tête à tête* ... or as you would say, face to face."

"And she will return your thanks, face to face. But in the meantime, these carriages are to transport you and your retinue to the Castle Royal. You will be escorted by these dozen knights led by Count Edgar of Ravenshead, here. Those five hundred foot-soldiers over there, led by my old comrade in arms, Baron Josiah Damrosch, will be here to attend to your rowers, and serve their needs. Already they have brought tents and food; their mission is to guard your men from discomfort and danger."

François glanced at the scowling hundreds of soldiers ready to surround them, all giving the impression that they would cheerfully obey a command to slaughter every single one, and he smiled wanly. "Keeping my rowers safe and comfortable, are they? *Quelle mission bénigne!*

General Lord Flexner smiled grimly. Although François had thanked him personally, Flexner had avoided returning his thanks. Did the French King notice? And did he notice that Sir Hubert, together with his sixteen rowers, had quietly slipped the longboat into the river and had quickly rowed away? *I don't give a damn whether he noticed anything or not,* Flexner thought; *I want to see what happens when he and Her Majesty meet, as we would say,* face to face.

By the time the bray of the long heraldic horns was heard in the Castle Royal, preparations were almost complete. The inner walls – those that the visitors would see, at any rate – had been scrubbed, guest quarters prepared, extra provisions brought in, and the evening banquet was almost ready to start cooking. Servants had fussed over Anna and Jane, grooming them and robing them exquisitely. This time Anna did not disdain makeup; she allowed her eyebrows to be darkened, and her lip color, already a sweet coral, to be subtly enhanced by lip coloring. She even allowed a slight spot of rouge to be rubbed into the flawless complexion of her cheeks. She donned the crown she had worn on her coronation, and Jane put on a golden tiara studded with pearls, so when they took their places on the dais in the Throne Room, they shone like the resplendent stars of the realm they were.

On both sides of the Throne Room, leaving a broad aisle through which the guests could approach, stood the nobility in order of rank (the highest ranks closest to the Queen); similarly in the courtyard all the servants lined the way from the portcullis to the inner gate (though in no particular order), so that everyone in the castle could have a chance to greet the royal visitor and his entourage.

Hearing François' arrival in the outer court, Anna's heart started to pound, and it beat wildly when the Lord Chamberlain proclaimed, "His Majesty, King François of Burgundy!"

Then she saw him, and her lips parted.

Oh my God ... she thought, *he's just like* him ... *whom I buried!* She trembled as he approached. But when he was closer she thought *no no,* of course *he's not* quite *like him; one can see the difference ... it's not obvious, but it's there.* And she felt a keen disappointment, almost a pain in her heart. *Why are you so let down,* she thought, *you fool! What did you expect – a miracle? Come on Anna – cheer up! You* can *tell the difference, and that's* good; *you don't want to seem like a crazy woman. He just hopes to shake you up a little. Well, let's just give him what he wants, shall we? We'll play the part of a stressed, shaken woman – which should be easy: It's close to the truth.*

When François neared the bottom step of the dais, He said "Greetings from France the fair to the Monarch who is fairer even than France. On the drive over, I asked the coachman to stop so I could pick some lovely flowers growing by the side of the road." He lifted his hand and an underling placed in it a bouquet, which he raised so everyone could see it, and he proclaimed, "I had thought these flowers beautiful until I saw you, Your Majesty, whose beauty puts them to shame! Still I hope you will accept them, as a token of my admiration and respect."

Anna thought: *His voice is not unlike Andrew's.* She rose from her seat. "You're most kind," she said. Then she turned to one of her own people and said "will you take these flowers from His Majesty and place them in a vessel of water? They will adorn our table at the banquet tonight." Then she turned back to François. "Your Majesty," she said, "I have heard that the French are very graceful with words, and you certainly live up to that reputation. What remains to be seen is whether your deeds live up to your words."

"Your Majesty," he said, "nothing would please me more than to show you the depth of my feeling – not only in words – but passionately, in *deeds*."

Anna felt herself blushing, and wanted to get out of there. "On that note," she said, let us adjourn and prepare for supper, which will be in the great hall in three hours."

The supper offered little more than the usual everyday fare served at the castle – A soup with chicken, herbs and spices, grilled wild boar, roast lamb flavored with ginger and cinnamon, loaves of bread in many shapes and sizes, and, at the end, apple pie with figs, raisins and spices. All this, of course, was accompanied by plenty of wine.

Anna was apologetic. "If we had known exactly when you were coming, Your Majesty, we might have tried for something special, instead of this hastily thrown together affair. Accustomed as you must be to exquisite French cuisine, this sorry spread must disappoint you."

"Au contraire, Votre Majesté, beaucoup au *contraire,"* François cooed. "What I see before me" – and here he looked directly at Anna, deep into her eyes – "is more than enough to whet my appetite."

What effrontery! Anna thought. *Andrew would never have dared to talk to me like that! – but of course, Andrew was only a Baron, whereas this man is a King, and is used to getting whatever he wants – unlike me.* What do I mean – *unlike me? I'm royalty too: I'm a Queen – don't I get what I want? Good question. But I must pay attention: This man thinks he's being gallant, and is gazing into my eyes almost the way Andrew used to, and he expects a response. I better say* something, *but what?* "You're too kind," she said finally, avoiding his eyes and looking demurely downward.

"I *want* to be kind to you," he answered, "but *too* kind? It is impossible to be too kind to such a one as you. But whatever little things I can do ... for example, these knives at your table setting, they are crossed – which is extremely bad luck. Let me fix them for you ..." And he uncrossed the knives and set them so that they lay strictly parallel to each other. "There!" he said, "all fixed. *Ma chère,* I want to fix *everything* for you."

He began to reach for her hand, but was interrupted by the breathless arrival of Lord Flexner, who looked directly at Anna. "Your Majesty!" he said, "something has happened that requires your immediate attention. If it please you, Ma'am, we should withdraw and consider it directly."

Anna turned to François almost with relief. "Forgive me, Your Majesty," she said, "but apparently there's business afoot that I must see to. But I'm sure you know how that feels."

"I do indeed," said François. "Take your time, *Votre Majesté*; the night is still before us." Whereupon Anna and Lord John left the banquet quickly, leaving her throne-like seat empty.

François had been placed to Anna's left. To the right of her throne-like seat, in a lesser throne of her own, sat Princess Jane. François looked at her and said, "Your Royal Highness, you take after your sister in two ways: First, you are very beautiful."

"Don't waste your gallantry on me, Your Lordship," Jane replied. "My heart is already given."

François' face gave no hint that he was displeased to hear Jane's deliberate slight in not addressing him according to his royal title. Instead he said, smilingly, "of course it is – and in that way you also take after the Queen your sister. For according to my sources, your chances of realizing your romantic dream are as unlikely to be realized as hers."

"I should hope they'd be better," said Jane. "My love, at least, is alive."

"For the moment, yes," François smiled. "But in these matters, things can change quickly – and without warning."

"I assume I may take that as a threat?"

"By no means, Your Royal Highness," François said smoothly. "All I mean is that you never can tell how fate will overtake those in high places. Her Majesty your sister never dreamed – after the death of the unfortunate Baron Steele, and after years of searching for him vainly in the dust – that at long length a new love would find her."

"You think she'll accept you? Really? I know Her Majesty, and I wouldn't be so sure of that."

At that moment Anna, closely followed by Lord John, strode up to where François was sitting. "Your Majesty," said Anna, "Lord John here has discovered something shocking." She turned to Lord John. "General Flexner," she said, please tell His Majesty what you found."

"Gladly ma'am." He turned to address the royal guest: "King François," he said, "right after you and your party arrived – seemingly in only those three ships, I dispatched Sir Hubert Brookford in a small longboat of our own to find out whether you hadn't really arrived with many more ships, most of which might be lurking out of sight beyond the horizon. He has just returned to tell us that yes indeed you do have more ships nearby – some five hundred of them!"

"Four hundred seventy-eight, to be exact," said François smoothly. "Yes, they're all mine."

"So, François of Burgundy," said Anna with a thin smile on her face, "is *this* is your offer: Love me *or else?* If I had rejected your suit, if I had said no to *anything whatever,* were you prepared to invade me with this vast armada? Is this your project then: not love, but conquest, to the pleasure of which you hope to add what joys you imagine in my bed?"

Anna's voice had so risen that by the end she was almost screaming, her words reverberating off the stone walls. All other conversations ceased, all other movement stilled, so that in profound silence everyone in the banquet awaited François' reply.

When that reply came, it came very quietly: "I was advised to take with me this armada, as you call it. For my protection."

"Hah!" This ejaculation escaped General Flexner's lips, but with a motion of her hand Anna the Queen silenced him.

"Do you think me a fool, François?" said Anna, "If we were to kill you right now, would your hidden ships save you? No. You hid them because you knew that once we saw them, we'd never let you land without a fight, and your romantic suit would be over before it began. But you figured that if you hid most of your ships, you'd be allowed to land peacefully, and you could begin the work of ... softening me up, as it were, so that the love-drunk Queen would be disinclined to refuse a few additional supply ships, as you would call them, then a few more, then a few more, until finally she'd be powerless to prevent the rest of the armada from descending on us like the killers they are, ending my reign and my life, then enslaving Grandlandia."

"You're not a fool, Anna," François said. "Something very much like that had been in my mind."

"Let me put an end to this, Your Majesty," Flexner said, drawing his sword. "Let me kill him now."

"No, Lord John," she said. "We could kill him now, but many others would take his place."

"Her Majesty is right," said the French King. "If you killed me, it would be only a matter of time before my grieving countrymen would swarm over Grandlandia like a horde of locusts, devouring everything – and every*one* – in their path."

"'Sblood!," cried Flexner. "Let me kill him."

"No," she said.

"Your Majesty," said François, "I seem to have underestimated you – grievously. I had supposed you were like the boring women I've met up to now – to be used and discarded. But you are anything but boring, and, to be honest, I'd like to know you better. I wouldn't blame you for not believing me; in your place I wouldn't believe me, either. But why not give me a chance to know you? Why not give yourself a chance to know me?"

"Why not?" Anna snapped, "that murderous armada over the horizon is why not."

"I'll send them back, then – every last one of them – back to France."

"Don't believe him, ma'am!" cried Flexner. "He's lying."

François took out an ornate blue and purple silk handkerchief, and patted his forehead with it. "Hold me hostage," he said, coolly, "and I'll write orders – under my seal – for the entire Armada. together with my entire entourage – every ship that came with me including the three berthed in Middleburgh – to return to France, and not return until three months from now. Let that sea-going Sir Hubert of yours accompany them. If, say, in a month, he doesn't return with news that he actually saw my fleet arrive in France, you can kill me – hopefully as mercifully as you can. That will be our arrangement."

"But no matter what happens," Anna said, the armada will return in three months, and we will be where we are now."

"Maybe not," François said. "Maybe you and I will know each other better, and if so, who knows what will have developed between us? One thing is for sure: You are a small country. We are three times your size," he said, folding his silk handkerchief with exquisite precision and tucking it delicately into one of the pockets of his robe. "It is natural for us to try to expand our power by swallowing you up. You may be able to stave us off for a bit – determined resistance can hold off a larger power for a while. Or you can make alliances with our enemies, deterring us that way. And you may be able to negotiate treaties whereby you retain the illusion of sovereignty while becoming in fact either our vassal, or someone else's. One way or another, in amity or in war, many non-Grandlandian ships are destined to visit you. It is up to you to determine how. It can be a project for us both to work on – jointly. Are you interested?"

Anna stood behind the throne-like chair, her hands resting on the two small crowns surmounting either side of the chair's back. *Killing him now,* she thought, *would be easy. But dealing with the consequences would be* anything but *easy. During the next few weeks, I can* always *kill him, but if I do, my options radically diminish. But if I listen to him, I still have my options, and possibly gain more, depending on what he says. Let's play along with him for a while and see where it goes.*

Anna looked up and saw that everyone in the banquet was waiting for her answer breathlessly, not daring to put down a fork. She looked at François. His life depended on her answer; she had better not make him wait any further: "Yes, *Votre Majesté,*" she said, "I am interested."

THIRTY-FIVE

For now, lie low.

When it was time to retire, François was led to a spacious Solar dominated by a massive bed, close to which was a single, bronze candlestick whose light, he felt, was barely enough for him to prepare for sleep. *Is this how they treat me?* he thought. But then he saw that lying nearby the candlestick were three more candles, as he had requested, and he felt much better. It wasn't that he was afraid of the dark – no, no, he kept telling himself. It was rather that he didn't especially *like* the dark, didn't like those uncomfortable moments before sleep where he would find himself staring into the blackness, looking for ... *what*? He was afraid to acknowledge what it was. Thus, when his eyes became accustomed to the candle-lit gloom, he became aware that there was someone sitting in the chair occupying a dark corner of the opposite far wall.

"Who's there?" he cried, reaching for his dagger. *If Flexner sent me an assassin,* he thought, *he's got a fight on his hands – they* both *do!*

"After all these years of our working together," said the shadowy figure, "you don't recognize me?"

"Vieuxtemps! How did you get in here? Are you working for *them*, now?"

"No, my liege. I've been working only for you – ever since your elder brother's death."

"I've asked you to stop bringing that up" said François, looking down. He then muttered, gazing at the floor, "I did not tell you to do that."

"Not in so many words."

"Not in *any* words, dammit!" said François, his voice rising.

"No, but you *thought* it," said Vieuxtemps, very quietly. "Guillaume was a dreamer; he was weak, ineffectual. So I got rid of him – paving the way for you, *Votre Majesté.*"

"I didn't ask for it," said François, sounding exhausted. "I never would have asked for such a thing, let alone do it."

"Of course not," Vieuxtemps said soothingly, "you never spoke the words. But all the same, you *wanted* it. And when you, *Votre Majesté,* want things, when you merely *think* things, I *do* them. It's very handy for you, even if I do say so myself, who shouldn't."

"Then why do you say it?"

"Because *you haven't.*"

"I haven't fired you; you should be grateful for that."

"Of course I am. Without your unspoken commands, what would I do for pleasure?"

"You got pleasure from all the spying and killing you've been doing over here?"

"Of course. It was what you wanted."

"I thought it was, but I've changed my mind."

"Really! When did *this* happen?"

"None of your business when it happened!"

"You don't have to tell me. It must have happened tonight. Dining with the beauteous Anna is enough to turn any man's head."

"Listen, Vieuxtemps: I don't want any more killing. I still want Grandlandia of course, but not to enslave its people, and certainly not to destroy its Queen. I want it for ... something else."

Vieuxtemps smiled knowingly. "Why don't you sleep on it and see how you feel tomorrow?"

"I will not be patronized by you! If you don't know your place, you can get the hell out of here! I don't need you, and I can do very well without you."

Vieuxtemps burst into a roar of laughter, but François was not amused. "What the hell are you laughing about?"

Vieuxtemps tried - not very convincingly - to contain his amusement, and said, together with irreverent giggles: "O most Puissant Master, thrust me not from you!" And he prostrated himself repeatedly before the King of France.

"Get up, fool," said François, "I will do nothing of the kind - provided that you hear what I'm telling you."

"Oh, I hear you."

"I wonder if you do. Tell me, Vieuxtemps, if, as you say, I really did thrust you from me, what would you do?"

"Well I'd ..." Vieuxtemps affected a melodramatic expression, beat his chest with his fist, and intoned, "I'd simply shrivel up and die - that's what I'd do."

"Nonsense. Be real."

"I *am* real. If you rejected me, *votre Majesté,* who knows what I'd do? I'd ... I'd ... I might even ..." Vieuxtemps clapped a hand to his forehead, and declaimed, "I'd simply cry and cry until I had no tears left, no *water* left, and then I'd die of dehydration!"

"I see I can't get a serious answer from you."

"Because I can't get a serious question from *you*, my liege."

"Then try this: If I give you a command, Hector, will you obey me?"

"My Liege Lord, I will do *only* what you want me to."

"Good," said François. "For now, lie low." Then he leaned close to his creature's ear. "I may have use for you in the future," he whispered, whereupon Vieuxtemps melted into the darkness. François heaved a sigh of relief, then allowed himself a faint smile.

Vieuxtemps, meanwhile, was threading his silent and shadowy way through the Castle Royal. If anyone had been unlucky enough to encounter him, it would have been too dark to tell whether Vieuxtemps' face was smiling or not.

THIRTY-SIX

The Commingling of Breaths

Lord John Flexner and his Lady Prudence had blown out the candles, but neither could sleep. Each was lying near their respective edges of the bed, leaving a chaste space between them.

"You were there," he said. "You saw him admit that his aim had been to conquer Grandlandia, murder Her Majesty, and enslave the country."

"I saw it."

"Twice I begged her to let me kill him, and twice she refused!"

"I saw that, too. But she said that had you killed him, we'd be in for a devastating attack in reprisal."

"You would think that by this time she'd believe in my ability to defend us!"

"Yes, but at what cost, My Lord? If François is right – if the force of numbers must overwhelm us in the end, is delaying our doom worth the sacrifice of so many people? That was probably on her mind."

"Maybe that – or maybe her unwillingness to see me kill someone who looks so much like her Andrew. That was probably it, don't you think?"

"What I think is that you're not giving her Majesty enough credit. She's a very smart woman."

"Don't you think I know that? I know she's got a brilliant mind telling her things, but her *heart* may be saying *don't listen, don't listen to what your mind is telling you!* Look: She's just heard a man confess his worst intentions, but scarcely a moment later he's saying, "let's get to know one another and see what develops!" And *she* says 'I'm interested!' How smart is *that?"*

"I grant you," said Prudence, "it doesn't sound very smart."

Lord John heaved a deep sigh. "It isn't," he said, "trust me."

"I do trust you, My Lord."

"You do? If so, you're the only one around here who does."

"I'm sure that's not true," Prudence said. "But right now, at this very moment, knowing who trusts you is less important than knowing whom *you* trust."

"Why is that?"

"Because you're in bed with someone, silly! If you want to get some sleep, you had better trust your bed mate not to harm you while you sleep."

"Now you're the one who's silly. You would never harm me."

"Of course I wouldn't. But if I wanted to, I *could."*

"What ideas you have in your head!"

"Many women have them. They just don't talk about them to men. Men have all the power, and too often they don't treat their women well; they abuse them. But while the men are sleeping, they're vulnerable, and abused women sometimes stay awake, dreaming of taking advantage of it."

"But you would never do such a thing, would you?"

For answer, Prudence said in a low voice, "Give me your hand, Lord Man-Mountain."

Flexner, who was to Prudence's right, extended to her his left hand, which she took in both of hers, and with all the tenderness that had been filling her for many months, she pressed her lips into his huge palm and kissed it, over and over. He found himself turning to her, his right arm reaching for her, and he rested his right hand on her shoulder.

"Now then, my love," she said in a throaty voice, "do you think I could do such a thing?"

"No Prudence, I could never believe that of you."

She sighed deeply. "That's because I could not – even if you were horrible to me, I could not."

He sighed, too. "Well at least *that's* settled. Now I can sleep." And he started to withdraw his left hand from both of hers, but she tightened her grip on it.

"Oh please, don't take your hand away," she murmured, "I like it."

"All right," he said, "that's all right." And with his free hand, he patted her shoulder.

And so the two of them fell asleep facing each other, their breaths commingling.

THIRTY-SEVEN

A Simulacrum of a Man

"What I don't understand," said Anna, "is how you could *think* of such a grotesque mission, let alone undertake it." She and François were walking in the garden situated behind the Castle Royal. They were surrounded by Flexner's soldiers, with the General himself in attendance, his sharp eyes and ears keenly alert for signs of danger. The military were far enough away so that if Anna and François spoke quietly, they need not be overheard.

"I am going to tell you the whole truth, *Votre Majesté;* to do less leads to unlucky things."

"Go ahead."

"I had told you, *Votre Majesté,* that as a young Prince, and even more so as a young King, I was drawn to women, and they were drawn to me, because power is arousing to women. And because power is corrupting to men, I tried to make a game of it; I wanted to see how many of them I could seduce. Like all men of power, I began to think I was entitled to the services of everyone in my realm, including all the beautiful women."

"I presume," said Anna, "that you did not reveal to your conquests-to-be the truth you just told me."

"Of course not! My success rate would have plummeted. As it was, however, one success followed another with predictable regularity: I was becoming bored – bored with the process, and bored with the result. I was considering swearing off women."

"Oh dear!" said Anna, laughing.

"But then someone told me that I had an uncanny resemblance to a courageous General in your army, someone you loved and for whom you were continuing to mourn. I started playing with the idea of offering myself as his replacement. Of course, I knew that I would have to overcome tremendous resistance; for someone in mourning, no one can *ever* take the place of the lost loved one. But in my favor would be my resemblance to the departed, and since grief can make one so ... *vulnérable* ... I figured I had a reasonable chance, and besides, *what did I have to lose?* Making the situation all the more *piquant* was the fact that for some time I had set my sights on Grandlandia as an easy conquest. Winning the widow would make the conquest much easier, indeed a pleasure."

"Your honesty is stunning, Your Majesty – and fascinating: While you made sure to withhold the whole truth from your prior conquests, from *me* you hold back nothing! Why is that?"

"If I said that I was tired of playing games, would you believe me?"

"No. Tiring of game playing is the last thing I'd suspect of you. On the contrary, I think you're playing a game right now, which is: Can you get this emotional woman to fall for you in spite of every disgusting detail you reveal to her? And can you do it in spite of the arrival, in three months, of an enormous fleet of ships, which would seem to add to the toxic stew the smell of coercion, saying in effect: *You better love me* or else."

"*Formidable!*" François cried. "Your way with words – *merveilleux!* There is nothing I could add to your presentation, except the fact that for the next three months, my life is in your hands. You can have me killed any time you want."

"And risk immediate war with a power three times our size? Yes, I have that option, and have not ruled it out."

"Well then, as you deliberate, I hope you'll consider my candor as evidence of my sincerity. Since my life is at stake, why would I risk it by telling you anything negative about me unless I aimed to begin as I hope to continue – with absolute honesty?" He smiled.

"Please don't do that," she said.

"Do what?"

"Smile at me like that. That's how Andrew used to look when he wanted to win me over."

"Tell me about him."

It was her turn to smile. "Not that he ever had to try that hard to win me. I was won from the first time I saw him. He felt the same way, but was very shy; I was his Queen, after all. He would never have made the first move, so I had to do it, and it's a good thing I did: The day after, he was killed ..."

Her eyes were tearing; François offered her his silk handkerchief, but she refused it and looked away. She did her best to continue: "I got General Flexner to place Andrew's body in the carriage with me, and I cradled him in my arms as we drove forward ... The arrow that killed him had been meant for me, and there was a good chance that a crossbow bolt would burst through the carriage and finish me off as well, but I didn't care; I felt that my life was over, anyway ... In a way, it *was* over. Andrew had been kind and gentle, yet very passionate, and he loved me for who I was as a person, not for what I could do for him as Queen. He was completely ethical, and he loved Grandlandia almost as much as he loved me. I knew I would never see his like again."

"He sounds like a beautiful man."

She engaged François' eyes with a gaze that was a challenge, and said, *"he was."*

"With all due respect to the dead," he returned, "may I ask if it's possible that had Andrew survived, and you and he married, might you have discovered in him flaws that would have made him seem a little more like a human being, and a little less like a god?"

"And with all due respect to *you, Votre Majesté*," she said, resisting the impulse to strike him, "is it possible that if *you* survive a few more weeks away from your flattering court, you might start to seem a little more like a real man, and a little less like a simulacrum of one?"

THIRTY-EIGHT

All you need do is give the order.

"General Flexner," Anna said, "you need worry no longer about my falling in love with François Rex. He's impossible – so full of himself that no one else can get in. I can hardly wait for him to return to France."

She was in her Council Room together with Flexner, Count Edgar, and Turco. On the council table the velvet coverlet had been removed from the cherry wood casket, which, touched as it was by a beam of light from the window, seemed to glow with an immanent power.

"*Must* he make it back to France, Ma'am?" Flexner said, smiling. "I can think of all sorts of accidents that could befall him."

Anna laughed. "So could we all, Lord John, and would to God we could get away with it! But we couldn't. François is our guest, and we are responsible for his safety. Even if he had a genuine accident, everyone would be convinced that it was regicide, and there'd be nothing we could do to change their minds. François knows this, and knows that we know it as well. He is not our hostage; we are his, and the threat of our decimation is his guarantee that we will keep him safe."

"Are you saying, Ma'am," said Flexner, "that we are doomed to lose any war we might have with the French, so that if they but raise their hand against us, we ought to surrender at once? I think we are better than that."

"Of course we are," Anna said, "much better. With your generalship, we could win many battles against them. But a whole war? Three to one? With such odds, I question it."

"Mere numbers are no sure indication of odds," Your Majesty. "We'd be fighting to defend our homes, our families. They'd be fighting merely for the expansion of empire."

"But what if they were fighting to avenge a martyred king," Anna said; "what if they were fighting to punish an ungodly Grandlandia for killing him? François' successor would whip his people into a frenzy of revenge, and would tell them that the dead king's bones had become sacred relics to be recovered at all costs. No matter what the problems were at home - corruption, famine, plague, whatever - the new king would distract the people with the lure of *holy war,* with immediate rewards of booty here on earth, and eternal rewards of salvation in heaven! And if they were unlucky enough to fail the first time, they'd come again, and again, and again. Holy wars don't end easily."

"Well said, Your Majesty!" said Count Edgar. "From this we can conclude that while François is in our custody, we must do our best to preserve him. But if he attacks us, *he's on his own.*"

Turco spoke up: "So it remains for us to figure out how to discourage François - once his fleet returns - from attacking. I don't mean promoting a marriage between him and Her Majesty - no Grandlandian wants that."

"Well," said General Flexner, during these next three months we could have constant military drills and practices - right under his nose. That ought to tell him *we are ready,* and indeed, would help ensure that we are."

"Great idea," Turco said. I wish I could be confident that drills and practices – by themselves – will be enough to make us seem unappetizing to him, and encourage him to direct his lust for conquest elsewhere."

"That would be a wonderful resolution," Anna said, "but our trouble isn't only his lust for conquest – it's his lust also for *me.* And I fear that if *that* lust is frustrated, it will feed his lust to conquer our country, however unappetizing and indigestible we try to appear."

"We certainly don't want you to appease his lust for you in any way," said Flexner. "That would be completely unacceptable."

"I agree," said Edgar.

"Absolutely!" said Turco.

"To suggest otherwise would be tantamount to treason," said Flexner.

"Well, as to that," said Anna, "it would be treasonous only if I myself didn't want him – which, at present moment, is an understatement."

Her three advisors sighed in relief.

Anna rose, causing her three counselors also to rise. "Gentlemen," she said, "We think this council meeting has helped clarify the issues for us, and has been very helpful. We are lucky to have you. We thank you all."

Once the three men had bowed themselves out of the room, Anna opened the rosewood casket, and was about to lift out the image within when Princess Jane rushed into the room.

"I have to speak with you," she said.

Anna quickly closed the casket, carefully draped its velvet coverlet over it, and took a deep breath. "Yes, dear?" she said.

"I can't stand being away from Emanuel. I want to start seeing him again."

Inwardly, Anna flared in anger. With everything she had to cope with, she felt she had neither the time nor the patience to deal with the demands of a impetuous teenager, especially her sister, who ought to know better. She opened her mouth to speak, then closed it again – experience had taught her not to say the first thing that came into her head. She thought it over: It wasn't so long ago that she herself was a teenager with the same longing – only with nobody in whom she could confide. She must not turn a deaf ear to Jane. But how could she do that and still shield her? "I know how you feel, dear," she said as sympathetically as she knew how, "but that murderous Vieuxtemps is on the loose, and I don't know how to give you what you want and still protect you."

"No need to worry, Anna: I've thought it all out and written it down – *here.*" And she handed Anna a piece of parchment with instructions written in a tiny, precise script. You can read it now, if you like."

Anna took the script and began reading, her eyebrows lifting as she made running comments: "You want us to ... You mean we're going to have to ... And you think they'll agree to ...?"

Jane spoke very calmly. "All will go very smoothly. All you need do is give the order."

"I'll do no such thing!" said Anna the Queen, finally beginning to give way to the frustrations and anxieties seething within her. "This plan is preposterous. You want us to go through all *that* for the sake of ..." She was going to say "an adolescent infatuation," but she held her tongue, leaving her sentence unfinished.

Jane finished it for her: "For the sake of love, yes: *Love.* Look, Anna: I've seen you with that Cherry Wood coffin, out of which you unearth Andrew's picture when you think nobody's looking, and then you commune with it. You were going to do that just now when I interrupted you. I don't blame you. It may well be – God forbid – that such a fate will be mine. But if it *is* mine, and there's nothing left of Emanuel except an image and some memories, I want to have more than one night of love to remember."

"How dare you!"

During the long silence that followed, Anna glared at Jane, who gazed back at her steadfastly. Finally Anna looked away. "All right," she said, "you'll get your way in this. You're my sister, and for your sake I should try any plan that has a chance of working. And this ... just might."

"Thank you," Jane said quietly.

"Don't mention it."

Jane turned to go, but at the doorway she turned to look at Anna. "By the way," Jane said, "I hope you've seen that there is no more open-door rule. That rule is *out.* Did you notice?"

"Yes, dear," said Anna. "I noticed."

THIRTY-NINE

So ... this is what it is!

And so it was that the next day, the word was given out that Princess Jane's maidservant, Hannah Moro, would have her quarters moved to a location adjacent to Princess Jane's. To accomplish this, a very large linen closet next to Jane's quarters would be converted into living quarters for Moro, with the added feature of a doorway inserted into the common wall between Moro's new quarters and Jane's. The purpose of this doorway, it was further given out, was to enable Hannah to serve the Princess more expeditiously. This would constitute a considerable promotion for Moro, since the linen closet was much larger than the tiny room she was currently occupying.

The day after that, six soldiers from Fort Steele arrived to begin the work, which began, modestly enough, with their moving the linens to another room in the castle. But then the hard work began, with the soldiers cutting through the stone in the wall that would be shared by Moro's new quarters and those of the Princess. The work was very hot and dirty, and soon the workmen were covered in stone dust. Princess Jane was very solicitous for their comfort, continually bringing them cold water to drink and sometimes moist cloths so they could wipe the dust and sweat from their faces. She was careful not to show any favoritism to any of these workmen, but one of them did notice that she lingered ever so slightly when she brought him his cup of water, and favored him by surreptitiously squeezing his hand when putting the damp cloth in it. This workman was, of course, Emanuel Agright.

Interestingly, the other five workmen knew who he was – no soldier at all, but the son of the late Viscount Albemarle Agright of Domeny. These five had been given strict orders by General Flexner to make sure that Emanuel had the toughest jobs in the project – a punishment they thought manifestly unfair, for though his father had been a notorious enemy of Her Majesty, Emanuel was admired for his gentleness and generosity, and well known for his continual praise of both Her Majesty and Her Royal Highness. It seemed clearly unfair to inflict manual labor upon one so undeserving and so gently reared. Emanuel, for his part, soldiered on stoically, performing these especially onerous tasks without complaint, and the other workers tried to assist him whenever they could. When they talked about it, they spoke in whispers, for General Flexner had warned them that if anyone found out who this "laborer" was, they would be demoted, and would suffer other punishments as well.

In a few days, a doorway was chiseled out of the common wall, a wooden door on leather hinges fitted into the doorway, the whole room washed down and swept up, and maidservant Moro's things brought up from her former room. There was no more work for five of the soldiers, but plenty of work – and heavy work at that – remaining for their erstwhile comrade, Emanuel, who was ordered to remain with the Royal Family as a sort of slave, the lowest among the low. When the soldiers bade him farewell, they commiserated with him about life's unfairness, and they hoped that his luck would change.

Hannah, meanwhile, had been telling everyone that there were ghosts inhabiting her room, also the Princess' room and the adjacent hallway. But not to worry, she said, for these spirits had shown themselves fearful of bell ringing. So anybody walking the halls near the Princess' quarters would often see Hannah ringing a bell, which, she insisted, was to scare away one particular ghost or another, which she would describe in dramatic – indeed scarifying – detail. Not coincidentally, all this occurred when Emanuel was with the Princess in her quarters.

The first time Emanuel made such a visit, he had come in from the garden, where he had been assigned the job of extending the garden's perimeter, turning over the earth with a crude spade, then carrying large stones away to the new perimeter.

He finished the job in mid afternoon, when the sun was still blazing. He went at once to the cool room where he knew Jane was waiting. He was dirty, sweaty, and understandably amazed when she announced, "here comes your reward for all that work," throwing herself into his arms. She kissed him passionately, he returned the kiss with fervor, and after a few minutes of their losing themselves in their embrace, her kissing stopped, for she was gasping in orgasm. When her throes subsided her eyes opened and she whispered, "so ... so ... this is what it is!"

"What is?" he asked.

"What just happened to me," she murmured. Whatever it is, I want more!"

By this time, Emanuel had caught on, and he took her hand and pressed it against his trousers, so she could feel his swollen penis underneath. "When we are married, he said, you'll get *this,* and you'll *have* more of what it is – as often as you like."

"Must we wait 'til then?"

"I want everything right between us. So much in the world is wrong, but in our home, it can be right; it *must* be right. Let's make sure that it is."

FORTY

Vous êtes très courageuse.

"This is Dolph's Hill," said Anna to François, standing on a high promontory overlooking a grassy plain. "This was the site of our first battle against the rebels. We won it, thanks to General Lord John Flexner of Nightwood here," she said, indicating the General, who was standing at the head of a large detachment of soldiers. At Anna's request for privacy, this Guard was standing at some remove, so they didn't hear Anna tell François: "But he wasn't a General then. In those days, he was Sir John Flexner. The fight was supposed to be led by General Andrew Steele."

"Where was he?" François asked.

"It's a painful story."

"I'm sorry."

"Why should you be? You haven't been here long, so you couldn't have known: People around here never mention Dolph's Hill in my presence."

"And yet you've brought me here."

"It's the first time I've been back since that day."

"You were here?"

"Yes, but not during the battle. Count Edgar and I arrived afterwards, expecting to find Andrew here – General Steele – but all we found were the ... the ... *remains* of the battle – all the dead, with their insignia and all – showing that our forces had won, but had moved on. I was relieved to see we had won, but deeply disappointed not to see Andrew, who had promised to meet me here. I had no way of knowing that he had never even made it to the battleground."

"Why not?"

There was a pause, then she cried, "Oh God, why have I come here?!" She covered her face with both hands.

"We can leave, if you like."

"And show myself a coward?"

"You have to be brave to come here?"

"I have to be brave to remember what happened here - and *why* it happened. Andrew should have been on hand for the battle, but he wasn't - and it's partly my fault. We got word there was going to be an attack on the Castle - and it was Andrew's idea to evacuate me, Jane, and our attendants to Count Edgar's estate. Now Edgar was perfectly capable of getting us there safely, but Andrew wanted to go with him. He said he had time both for that and for getting to Dolph's hill on time, but Flexner warned him it was unlikely because he'd have to travel through the woods on a very dark night. Andrew wouldn't listen; he claimed that he had time enough for both, but the real reason was that ... he loved me, and was unwilling to part with me until he actually saw me safe at Edgar's place."

"How is this also your fault?"

"Because I was his Queen, and I could have commanded him to listen to Flexner - but I was unwilling to do that, and I persuaded myself that maybe he did know what he was doing ... because I loved him too and didn't want to part with him, either. So he tried to make it through the woods at night and got badly lost and arrived at the hill too late to fight the battle, too late to meet me who followed after, but just in time to encounter one of the chief rebels, the Earl of Jorelemende, Lord Halle, who had him tortured badly – so horribly that he couldn't lead in the final battle—"

"In the Field of Tears," François interrupted, "I've heard of that one."

"Yes, that one! He should have led there, but wasn't strong enough, and so stayed back with the baggage ... and with me. The arrow that got him had been aimed for my carriage. Had he not been weakened by torture, he wouldn't have been back with me, but in the forefront, leading ..."

"Where he also could have been hit," François said gently, "maybe even more likely so."

"The horses drawing my carriage were not battle hardened," she said, "and they reared up, out of control, so poor darling Andrew ran to them and pulled on the harness to steady them, and that's where he was killed – trying to save me!" During this last, Anna found it increasingly difficult to speak, and finally broke down, sobbing.

François held her. "Don't blame yourself, *ma chère amie,* don't blame yourself! What you did, you did for love, and so did Andrew. If I had been in his place, I would have done the same thing."

After a time, Anna tried to gain control of herself, very gently disengaging herself from François' embrace, and drying her eyes. "I apologize for this display," she said, looking away. "What must you think of me?"

"Vous êtes très courageuse," he said.

She looked at him.

"You are very brave."

"I'd like to think of myself that way," she said. "Maybe that's why after all these months I came up here today. Maybe that's why I brought *you*."

At that moment, a company of soldiers marched onto the grassy plain below, and proceeded to execute a series of phalanx maneuvers with coordinated lance throwing, followed by demonstrations of close combat with sword and shield, then by demonstrations of accuracy using the long bow, and finally by some virtuosic demonstrations of cavalry, complete with horse and rider leaping over formidable obstacles. That done, they formed themselves in ranks, faced the hill and bowed to the visitors above, all of whom – including François – applauded mightily. Then Anna waved to the soldiers below, causing them to break into cheers.

François turned to her, smiling. "What was that?" he said.

"It's General Flexner's idea of entertainment."

"Entertainment?"

"For us both."

"I think it was mainly intended to impress *me – non?*

"And were you impressed?"

"Certainement," he said, "but I can think of ways I'd prefer to spend my time. The highlight of my visit so far, *par exemple,* was just now when I held you in my arms."

"Well, you mustn't do that again – it shakes me."

"Shakes you? But why?"

She reached up and touched his beard, then gave him a quizzical smile. "Because I buried you," she said.

FORTY-ONE

She let him!

He held her, and she let him," said Lord John Flexner to his Lady, Prudence, when they were alone in their room late that night. "I couldn't believe it: After virtually swearing to us that she hated him, there she was in his arms! My worst fears were being played out right in front of my eyes, and I could do nothing about it. I kept hoping I'd wake up. "

"To feel so helpless – how hard that must have been for you!"

"It was. For some reason, she had burst into tears just before, and I felt powerless to help her."

"Why was she crying? Had he said anything to her?"

"I couldn't tell; they were too far away. But we did hear her sobbing, and we looked at each other; this was the first time any of us had seen Her Majesty act like that – usually she is so self possessed – and to see her break down so ... I wanted to run to her, comfort her, but there *he* was, drying her eyes with that damned silk handkerchief of his, and she let him!"

"Extraordinary!" Prudence said. "And you say she allowed him to hold her – meaning that she didn't return his embrace – right?"

"Not that I could see."

"Which suggests that she was passive about the whole thing, right?"

"I guess so."

"How did the embrace end?"

"Let me think ... now that I remember it: She put her hands up to his chest, and he backed away."

"Well, now!" Prudence said smiling, "that puts a different complexion on the whole thing. What I've heard does not sound at all like Her Majesty has fallen for the French King. It sounds like something made her cry; she needed comfort, and François was standing right there, so he comforted her. The question is, what made her cry? Do you think François did?"

"If so, she wasn't angry at him, for they watched the martial display standing very close together – too close together, in my opinion."

"Then it must have been something Her Majesty was thinking. It probably had to do with Lord Steele. Dolph's Hill, you remember, was where Lord Steele was taken by Lord Halle, who tortured him so badly he never really recovered."

"I know," said Flexner, "he couldn't lead the fight in the Field of Tears, but had to hang back with the baggage. That's where that arrow got him. As for his torture, I *warned* him to let Edgar escort Her Majesty to safety and not try to go with them; there wasn't *time* for him to escort Her Majesty *and* be ready for the battle at Dolph's Hill – it was impossible! Still, he wouldn't listen; it was his own fault that Halle caught him."

"However that may be," Prudence said, "Her Majesty blames herself. Standing on Dolph's Hill brought all of it back, and she started to cry."

"You think that was it?"

"Listen, My Lord: If someone you loved died because of a fault you imagined in yourself, wouldn't *you* feel like crying?"

"It's hard to say. I haven't cried since I was a small boy."

"But surely you must have *felt* like it, haven't you?

Flexner nodded wordlessly.

"Well then, remember Her Majesty up on that hill, she's with scores of her people; they all wish her well – yet she feels desperately alone. Yes, she asks for counsel and she gets advice, but in the end it is she who has to make the decisions, and the only person she would have relied on to share that burden is dead and buried."

Flexner frowned and started to move away, but Prudence brought him up short: "Look, John," she said. You know what it is to lead thousands into battle, knowing that some of them are going to die. Is there anyone you can ask, *am I doing the right thing?*"

"No. You have to do the best you can, and hope that it's good enough."

"A lonely feeling, right? Her Majesty feels the same way. But unlike you, when she feels like crying, sometimes she allows the tears to flow."

There was a long pause, and then Flexner said, "Lady Alder, I wonder what I would do without you."

"I hope you'll never find out," she said, giving him a hug.

General John Flexner of Nightwood found himself hugging her in return, and patting her affectionately.

FORTY-TWO

I'll know.

As François approached the entrance to his guest quarters, he steeled himself. Although he thought it unlikely that he would find Vieuxtemps in there – he hadn't appeared since the first night – one could never be too careful. After seeing that assassin his first night in Grandlandia, he hadn't slept very well, and he resolved to check carefully the next time he entered his room. Of course his nemesis wasn't there the first time François tried this, and on the superstitious theory that it seldom rains when you bring raingear, François determined to look for him *every* time he entered, supposing that maybe his continual looking out for him might somehow keep him away. So when he entered his quarters on the fourth night of his visit, and when he glanced purposefully at that dark corner where Vieuxtemps had appeared, but nevertheless saw him smiling there, he was visibly shaken.

"What?" said Vieuxtemps, "you weren't expecting me?"

"Oh I was, I was," François said. "I knew you'd come back *sometime.* I just had supposed it wouldn't be so soon. I don't have any business for you right now."

"Well, that's a problem isn't it? I'm bored."

"Do some *good,* for a change," François said.

"Let others stoop to that, if they like. It's not for me."

"Well, as I said, I have no work for you."

"Oh come on! I know that General Flexner irritates you. He was cold to you the moment you got here. And I'm sure he's not thrilled about your courting Queen

Anna. Possibly he senses the threat you pose to the country. More than that, I think he's in love with her himself."

"Well, who wouldn't be? She's a glorious woman and a very beautiful one besides. She's fit for a Prince."

"You sound like you're in love with her yourself."

"Yes, I do, don't I? Well it's about time I tried someone really worthy of me. This woman could be my Queen."

"General Flexner could be your rival."

"Not a chance. She wouldn't look at a mere Baron. She needs a Prince and I think she knows it."

"Well *I know you* as well as I know myself, Your Majesty. I know you're thinking that you'd have clearer sailing with Flexner out of the way."

"Listen to me, Vieuxtemps: Things are going very well for me now. Anna seems more and more comfortable with me, and I'm sure that my resemblance to her late love doesn't hurt. What *would* hurt is gratuitous violence on your part. She would freeze up, and then I might as well be at war with her. I'm telling you, Vieuxtemps, lie low. I'll tell you when I need you."

"You won't have to, Your Majesty. Just think your thoughts: I'll know."

FORTY-THREE

Ever'thin's fine, mum.

The villagers in Appleville hadn't seen a monarch in quite some time, having been visited ten years ago by the late, unlamented Queen Thanata of the man-eating moat. Why had she come? Nobody knew, and nobody dared ask – they were too frightened. So when Anna the Queen and her royal guest François rode in, complete with an escort of twelve knights led by General Flexner, the villagers were terrified. They stood frozen in little groups, silent. Sensing their fear, the children stopped playing and stared, while the mothers did their best to hush their squalling babes in arms.

But unlike Queen Thanata, who had been off for a joy-ride through the countryside and had thought it might be amusing to ride through a humble village, Anna and François actually dismounted, handing off the reins to a couple of uniformed equerries.

"Is there no one here willing to greet us?" Anna called out.

There approached a toothless old man leaning on a stick even more bent than he. "Welcome to our little hamlet, yer Majesty," he said. "This is an honor."

"Thank you," Anna said.

"With all due respect," said the old man, "may I ask why ye've come?"

"We've come to see how you're faring, goodman – to learn how life's been treating you."

"Oh! Well, as to that, ever'thin's fine, mum, as ye kin see ..." With his stick he gestured expansively. "Look aroun – ever'thin's lovely."

Anna looked at the scantily thatched roofs, and the emaciated children dressed in rags, and said, "things don't look all that lovely to me."

"Well, as to that, mum, we know we're poor, but we don't complain, we know what ye done for us, and we're grateful."

"We know what we *tried* to do," Anna said, "but looking around, we can't see that it has done all that much good."

"Well, speakin' a that, mum, it *was* better for a while, but then the Baron went back to 'is old ways – not that we're complainin' or nothin' – but seed prices shot up, and he started payin' us not much more than dirt for our barley, like he did before, don't ye know. But we understand; it's the way o' the world, I guess, and what are we gonna do? We take what we kin get, and we're grateful."

"We thank you for telling us, goodman," said Anna the Queen, "and we'll see what we can do. We can't promise anything, of course, but you've seen that we hate oppression, and we'll do our best to relieve it."

"Yer a noble soul, Yer Majesty, and we're yer 'umble servants," said the old man, removing his hat and going down on one knee, causing all the other villagers to do the same.

Anna walked to her mount, and, declining her equerry's offer of assistance, swung nimbly into the saddle, as did François, who still had not grown used to her graceful athleticism. She turned to the crowd of villagers and called out, "all of you please rise," and they all did, hat in hand, as they watched the Royal party ride off.

"First-rate public relations, *Votre Majesté*; they love you!" François said.

"I hope they do," said Anna, "but it wasn't just public relations: I meant it. This is what caused the rebellion."

"The peasants rebelled?"

"No – the landowners did, once they saw I wouldn't put up with their rapacious greed. Of course, not every landowner acted like this. There were exceptions, and those exceptions ultimately saved my throne. But the ringleaders of the rebellion – well, they got what they deserved. I tried them and had them put to death. The lesser leaders I punished – but not severely enough, apparently. A few months ago, I got word that their excesses had grown back like warts, and I knew I had to do something about it."

"And did you?"

"No, unfortunately I did not, because by that time your messenger had arrived with that picture of Andrew – well, you *claimed* it was of *you*—"

"And as you can see," said François, interrupting, "I was telling the truth."

"I haven't sorted that out yet. Please let me continue."

"Pardonnez moi."

"What I was trying to say was that I so preoccupied by the thought that someone like Andrew – someone who *looked* like Andrew – was coming, that I didn't follow through on redressing the peasants' grievances. I didn't do my job, and I have nobody but myself to blame for it. Still, in addition to all this, just about then we got word of a nameless assassin – someone claiming to be acting on your behalf: You remember: In a message you told us his name: Hector Vieuxtemps. We hear he's been murdering scores of our people with impunity, it seems; no one's been able to catch him."

"Not even General Flexner?"

"I *said* no one. Anyway, people are afraid to go out nowadays, and what with all this, I felt it was the wrong time to try to impose limits on aristocratic greed - *again.* Doubtless you're acquainted with this sort of thing?"

"Oui, vraiment!" he cried, *"la noblesse* constantly tries to undercut me, limit my power. With them I have my hands full!"

"And yet you find time to court the ladies - even going overseas to do so."

"Well, one must never forget what's most important in life, *non?*"

"Oui, vraiment!" she cried, with just a faint smile on her face. "But to *know* what's most important in life - that's the trick."

"You're saying you don't know this?"

"I thought I did. But now I'm not so sure."

FORTY-FOUR

It could go either way.

The Metaphysical Society of Grandlandia met monthly at the Castle Royal – not at the Grand Cathedral. This was partly because the huge size of the Cathedral dwarfed people and intimidated them – as it was designed to do. But the most important reason was the Society's mission: to explore what invisible connections might underlie the reality observable in the world, and to see how these invisible connections might guide one's actions and help one live more effectively. But the Archbishop regarded the Metaphysical Society's mission as subversive, even heretical, since he and his prelates already thought they *knew* what underlay observable reality, which was of course explained by the dogma put out by the Church, and which was not subject to debate or discussion.

Therefore the members of the Society thought it prudent to meet in secret, indeed to keep their very membership secret. Of course the Archbishop knew, in a general way, that these meetings were taking place, but since the Society made a point of discussing its ideas only among its members, and of limiting the membership to those men who attained a certain level of maturity and social standing; and since – and this was the most important thing – *the Society had the protection of Her Majesty,* the Archbishop thought it wise to leave it alone. If it became a danger to the Church, he could always stamp it out, he supposed, regardless of Her Majesty.

The Society had been founded, naturally, by an adept in these matters, Lord Turco, who moderated its meetings. And it was after the most recent of these, when the members had disbanded, that Lord Flexner caught sight of the metaphysician on his way out.

"Turco! Turco! What's the rush? Wait up, please, My Lord!" Flexner called, whereupon Turco duly turned to exchange pleasantries with the General. "My Lord," said Flexner, "we used to see you almost daily here in the Castle, but now only Her Majesty's council and these metaphysical meetings get you out of your house. Home life, I take it, is your most compelling attraction?"

"What else could rival it – other than Her Majesty, of course? But you, My Lord, should know this very well, being newly married just like me."

"You call yourself newly married, Turco? It's been more than three years!"

"It *feels* like we married yesterday," said the metaphysician. "Everything is still fresh and new. What happened was that I took my own advice, focused on *why* I fell in love with Angelina in the first place, and now ... OH! I can scarcely wait to see her, to touch her hand, to ... but I need not tell all this to you, My Lord; you must be having the same experience."

"Well, perhaps it's not quite so ecstatic as yours," said Flexner, "but I have to admit that I am enjoying it far more than I would have thought possible for a man like me."

"A great start, and let me tell you, My Lord, it just keeps on getting better and better."

"If you are any example, Lord Turco, then I'm sure it will do so for me as well. But it's not marital matters that I want to talk to you about, My Lord.

"Something else?"

"That's right. Do you remember that Council meeting where we first learned of King François' romantic overtures to Her Majesty?"

"Quite clearly."

"Do you remember that Her Majesty became so angry she virtually started screaming?"

"I'll never forget it."

"And do you remember you proposed that Her Majesty actually *invite* François over here, and on his arrival pretend that she is emotionally shaken by his resemblance to Lord Steele, but feels torn about it for obvious reasons? And that at the crucial moment, whenever that would be, our Queen, like some player in a chess game, would somehow *make her move* – those were your words, whatever they might mean? Do you remember any of that, My Lord?"

"I remember all of it, distinctly. I also remember how passionately you denounced this idea as subjecting Her Majesty to unnecessary risk."

"I still feel that way. And what I want to ask you, my dear Master of Metaphysics, is how's the chess game going? Who's winning, do you think?"

Turco paused, then smiled patiently at Flexner. "From what I've observed, General, it's too soon to tell. They're both positioning themselves adroitly, and in my opinion, it could go either way. But what do *you* think?"

"I think that François is crafting an emotional net meant to draw Her Majesty in, and that she will succumb to his blandishments and be netted – trapped."

"Well, I agree that an emotional net is being fashioned. But which of them will be netted is not quite so clear. It could just as well be François. But if Her Majesty is netted and *he* wins, his obvious move is to marry her and rule Grandlandia."

"Sure," said Flexner. "And if *she* wins, she can't have him killed – she's made that abundantly clear, and I think she's right. But if she can't have him killed, what *can* her move be?"

"I don't know," said Turco, "and at this stage of the game, she may not know herself. But have patience."

"PATIENCE? You're so goddam cool about this, Turco! Don't you know that how it turns out will affect Angelina's life and yours – not only that but the lives of everyone in the country? That we all face possible slavery or death?"

"I know it all too well, my Lord. But I also know that right now, having patience is the only thing that I personally *can* do."

"How long will we have to wait?"

"I don't know that either. But possibly, it may be sooner than we think."

FORTY-FIVE

I never gave those orders.

"Finally we are alone," Anna said to François. They were sitting next to each other in Anna's royal suite, she in a throne-like chair, he in a chair of lesser proportions. "It's hard to believe," she said, "that we're no longer being watched, reported on, and speculated about."

"Oh, we are still being speculated about, *Votre Majesté,* more intensely than ever, I should think. They just can't *see* us. Which means that there are a lot of frustrated people out there."

"Good! Why should we be the only ones?" said Anna.

"Are you frustrated as well, *ma chère amie?"*

Anna changed the subject. "These shoes are pinching me," she said, bending over sharply to remove them. When she sat up again, there was a flush on her face.

"May I hope that your blush speaks your reply?" said François.

"You may hope whatever you like," said Anna primly, "but I ... cannot deny that I've been longing for what I never can have – Andrew's kiss."

"*Ma cherie,* do not say you can never have it. I am here to supply it."

"What ... *you?* You could never do that. You merely *look* like him. Kissing your lips would be no more satisfying than kissing his picture."

"How do you know? You haven't tried it."

There was a silence, Then she said, "Fair enough." And with her arms still at her sides she leaned toward him, and he toward her. They kissed – tentatively, it seemed, then she broke away. "Interesting!" she said.

"Comment est-ce intéressant?"

"I felt as if I were detached from myself, watching me kiss someone who looked like Andrew. Not that it was unpleasant – not at all. It just felt ... strange."

"Perhaps a second try, Anna? To do one of anything is to court bad luck."

"Really! You're a bit on the superstitious side, aren't you?"

"More than a bit. But I find that superstition never hurts, and in fact may help."

"Well," she said, "as a sop to your superstition and to placate my own curiosity, let's give it another try," and she leaned again toward him, then with both hands she drew his head to hers, kissing him vigorously and at length. Finally she broke from him, breathing hard. "Ah, that was better – much better," she gasped.

"Maybe some more clothes are pinching, cherie? We could remove them as well."

"Oh God! Lord Flexner would have a fit if he knew."

François frowned. Then he muttered, "no no – forget I thought that. I don't want that."

Anna looked at him, genuinely interested. What don't you want, *Votre Majesté?* Have you changed your mind?"

"Never, cherie, I still want you, more than ever; pay no attention to what I said."

"But it's too late; I *have* paid attention, *mon ami,* and I need to know what thought you need forgotten, and what it is you don't want."

"If I told you, you wouldn't believe me."

"Try me."

"I have an assistant who reads my mind."

"Truly?" she said, disbelief on her face. He actually knows what you're thinking?"

"Vraiment!" he said, at least it *seems* that way. He knows me so well that he's sort of an alter *égo,* he knows what I want sometimes before even *I* know it – and then, without asking my permission he goes ahead and does it."

"Well, maybe that could be a good thing ..." Anna ventured.

"I suppose it could, but in my case it is almost always bad, sometimes horrible. The only good thing about it – if there could be a good thing – is that I can tell myself that I never actually gave the order for it. To the whole world, it seems like it simply happened – *somehow."*

There was a silence.

"Oh my God," Anna breathed, turning pale. "*Vieuxtemps* – he's yours."

"I'm afraid so."

"And all these murders – *your* doing."

"I never gave those orders."

"Tell me: What dastardly act did your mind think of a moment ago, and then retract? Tell me right now!"

"Well you had said that Lord Flexner would be upset, and for a moment—"

"Oh my God – John! She rose. "François," she said, "get out of here."

"But I didn't really want—"

"Get out!"

"And let Vieuxtemps come between us? I wish he were dead!"

"GET OUT RIGHT NOW! I've got to warn John!"

FORTY-SIX

The next move is yours.

When General Lord Flexner strode into Fortress Andrew, one of his lieutenants hurried to him, saluted and said, "we got your message, sir, so we let Lady Alder go with the messenger to another safe house."

"What the ...!" Flexner ran to the quarters he shared with Prudence, only to find her gone, and on the bed a parchment scroll, which read:

> *Greetings, my dear General. I am taking your beloved wife to the home of the late Viscount Agright of Domeny. I will install her there on the second floor – suitably bound, of course – and will be waiting for you on the first floor. If you do not arrive* alone *before midnight, tonight, I will set fire to the place, and she will be consumed in the resulting funeral pyre, or, to change the metaphor, she'll be a sacrifice on the altar of love. Funeral pyre? Altar of love? Maybe the same thing?*
>
> *The next move is yours.*
>
> —*Vieuxtemps*

Flexner rushed out of there and headed toward the stables, but was halted by a royal courier who thrust into his hand a message which read: "Dearest Lord John, you are in mortal danger from Vieuxtemps. I hope this reaches you in time. *Anna Regina.*"

"Please thank her Majesty and tell her I'll be on my guard," said Flexner, who then resumed his run toward the stables. But as he ran, he fixed Anna's words, "Dearest Lord John," in his heart as a talisman, and as an augur of success in the coming struggle.

Once in the saddle, Flexner urged his Destrier Ares into a full gallop, in which the magnificent stallion seemingly took great delight, so eagerly did he respond to Flexner's encouragement. But while Ares was enjoying himself, his rider soberly focused on the task ahead of him. Vieuxtemps' kidnapping of Prudence seemed obviously an attempt to force Flexner into a compromising situation. Who knows what awaited him when he went through the door. *But which door?* He wondered. From his recent assault on that house Flexner remembered that there was not only a front door, but a back door and side door as well. *Which should I choose – the front door? Wouldn't that be the one I'd be* expected *to use? Or might Vieuxtemps expect me to avoid the obvious entry and try the side or back door, leaving the front door less guarded? By that logic, wouldn't the front door be my obvious choice after all – unless Vieuxtemps anticipated my thinking and guarded the front – as I would have expected him to do in the first place?*

What with Are's plunging gallop and his own circular thinking, Flexner blinked his eyes lest he become dizzy. *I've got to wait until I see the place again,* he thought. *The circumstances – the light, or lack of it – might have the final say on all this.*

In thirty minutes, Flexner saw what he had to work with. It was dusk, and the stiffening breeze caused the shadows of the branches to move back and forth across the front of the house like spectral hands, feeling for a way to get in. *The front won't work for my entry,* he thought. *With the sunset behind me, my shadow will announce me like a thunderclap.*

He decided to explore further on foot, and looked for a tree to which he might tie Ares. Since it looked like a storm was approaching, the tree couldn't be too large, lest it attract lightning. Nor could it be too close to the house, lest Are's whinnying alert Vieuxtemps. He found an approximately twenty-year-old tree that seemed right, dismounted and tied Ares to it. "See you in a while, lad," he told his horse, patting him on the shoulder. The animal whinnied as his master jogged away into the descending darkness, and it occurred to Flexner that nobody in that house would be able to hear anything outside except the howl of the rising wind.

As he approached the rear, there was barely light enough for him to see that the door was hung on leather hinges. With his knife, he cut those hinges away, then maneuvered the door out from the grip of the latch holding it on the other side. Now it was totally free, and he placed the door carefully, quietly, to the side. Across the doorway there was a beam meant to keep the door from being opened inward. Flexner lifted it out of its iron brackets, and placed it to the side, next to the door. By this time, night had completely fallen, and the stormy sky allowed no moon or star light to relieve the absolute blackness. Feeling for the door opening, Flexner very carefully stepped in, and as he did there was a brilliant flash of lightning, accompanied almost immediately by a colossal crash of thunder. And in that blinding flash he thought he saw, standing at the other side of the room, the slight, sinewed form of Hector Vieuxtemps. Then he heard a voice: "Welcome, my colleague in killing, welcome to my current abode. I won't be here long, but you will be – until they find your charred corpse, that is. As soon as I kill you, I'm going to set fire to this place. I won't have to kill Lady Alder; she's tightly bound so that the fire will kill her for me – unless of course you'd prefer that I finish her as an act of mercy, so she won't have to endure the agony of being burnt alive. But why don't you call up to your lovely Prudence, so she can hear your voice while she's still has a chance to?"

But Flexner did not speak, since he knew that doing so would give away his position, which he was busy shifting while Vieuxtemps was talking. By this time the rain was falling heavily, so Flexner thought that perhaps Vieuxtemps would not be able to hear the sounds of his bumping into furniture as he moved across he stone floor, nor the sound of his sword being withdrawn from its leather scabbard. He thought, *I just need that bugger to keep on talking 'til I know where he is – and that shouldn't take long!"*

Vieuxtemps obliged him: "Depriving your darling of your voice, are you – or are you simply depriving me of your location? No matter."

But it did matter. Flexner felt sure he was within sword's length of Vieuxtemps, and he swung his sword murderously at the point where he felt sure Vieuxtemps was.

But precisely as Flexner's sword was beginning its swing, there was another flash of lightning which revealed Vieuxtemps in the act of leaping back. *What?* Flexner thought, *can this son of a bitch see in the dark?* It was too late to check his swing, so with nimbleness surprising in a man of his great size, he spun in the direction of the sword swing as he crouched low, and then, coming out of the crouch, sprang at the last place he had seen his enemy – and found him! – but lost him again, having in his grip only a fragment of cloth ripped from Vieuxtemps' tunic as the Frenchman spun away. And as he spun away he delivered on Flexner's left upper arm a punch that would have shattered the bone of a lesser man. It hurt the man-mountain, but his bone was still whole, and he could still fight.

"I could have broken that arm if I had wanted to," Vieuxtemps said as if reading his thoughts, "but I didn't want to end the fight so soon. Why spoil my fun?"

He uses words as weapons, Flexner thought. Another flash of lightning revealed Vieuxtemps some ten feet opposite him, in the martial artist's semi-crouch, ready to defend or attack.

In the blackness, Vieuxtemps' insinuating words oozed like oil: "My dear General, how fitting, how poetically *just* is this our first and last meeting. You, always the staunch defender of Her Majesty, now learn too late that she has turned against you. Queen Anna wants you dead, my poor fellow."

Nice try, you son of a bitch, but it won't work, Flexner thought. *She would never think such a thing.*

"Oh, wouldn't she?" Vieuxtemps purred, "I can read minds. And I know that we both are under sentence of death from the people whose approval we need the most Remarkable! It's another thing we two killers have in common. How does that make you feel?"

Does Anna really want me dead? Flexner thought as he shifted his position. *I've certainly given her enough grief. With me dead, she can do what she wants. Still, she wrote 'Dearest Lord John.' Are these the words of a woman who wants me dead? No – I won't buy it! But I'll just let that slime bag think that I do.* He loosened his grip on his sword and allowed it to fall on the stone floor with a reverberating clang, alerting Vieuxtemps to his new position. He said to him: "She wants me dead, does she? Then come get me, my good friend, and put me out of my misery." A brief flash of lightning showed Vieuxtemps coming straight at him in a flying kick.

That was all Flexner needed. He batted the kick away, causing Vieuxtemps to crash into him. With both hands he gripped his enemy around the neck and squeezed with all his might as he held Vieuxtemps away from him at arm's length. Vieuxtemps savagely chopped at Flexner's left forearm, breaking it. With a blow weaker than the first, he punched the other forearm, which did not break. He continued with kicks growing ever weaker, and the man-mountain, in ever increasing pain, held on and continued to hold on even though his sense of smell told him that Vieuxtemps' loosening sphincter had released his bodily waste. But still he held on until a faint flicker of lightning from the departing storm showed him his enemy's face – a death mask of malice and – interestingly enough – surprise. He let him drop, and immediately gripped his broken left arm with his right.

By this time the night sky was beginning to clear, and there was enough moonlight coming in for him to make his way to the bottom of the stairs. "PRUDENCE!" he cried. A muffled sound from the second floor encouraged him to go up the stairs, where he found his lady, bound and gagged. He managed with one hand to untie the gag.

"My darling," she cried, seeing the impossibly bent angle of his left forearm, "he hurt you!"

"I've had worse," he grunted. "But if you can roll to your side, I'll try to untie this rope, which he seems to have been knotted behind you." And so, working together, they managed to get her untied, whereupon he grabbed his left forearm again, feeling about to faint from the pain.

"This is terrible," she said. "Don't move. Let me see if I can find anything to help." And with that, she got up and searched the house, finding downstairs a two-foot long fragment of wood that might serve her purpose. She brought it upstairs.

"What are you doing?" he managed to get out.

"Quiet – save your strength. I'm helping." She then removed her garment and ripped from it a couple of long strips of cloth. With one she bound the two-foot long wooden fragment to Flexner's forearm, and with the other she created a sling to support the splint she had made for him. She then put on what was left of her garment again. "Now then," she said, "if I help you, do you think you can get up?"

He nodded, she helped him up, and they both made their way downstairs, and out the front door. "Ares!" he called, and the answering whinny from the horse told them which way they should go. When they finally made it to Ares, the stallion reared up ecstatically, but Flexner managed to calm him.

Prudence approached him slowly, and stroked his nose. "Now," she said to the man-mountain, "How are we going to get you up there?"

"We'll see," said Flexner. "Prudence, if you'll move back some ten feet or so, we'll try something." Prudence complied, whereupon Flexner, with his good hand, pointed to the ground and said, "Ares, lie down." With widened eyes, Prudence saw Ares lie down as commanded, and though one arm was broken, Flexner was able to climb into the saddle. "Now then, Prudence," he said, "first untie Ares, then approach us very slowly, and climb up behind me."

And while Flexner kept saying, quietly, "steady Ares, steady," Prudence climbed up as instructed, putting her arms around Flexner's waist.

Flexner said to Prudence, "hold on tight, now." And then to Ares he said, "Up, Ares, UP!"

And Ares stood up.

"Amazing!" said Prudence. "How did you get him to do that?"

"With a great deal of patience; it took a lot of time."

"Where did you find it – the time, I mean?"

"I didn't have much of a social life. He was my best friend – until I met you, that is."

And so, under a full moon and a sky radiant with starlight, they made their very slow way back toward Fortress Andrew. They spoke about the recent struggle; she related how Vieuxtemps, true to form, had told her every detail of his plot to kill Flexner, and how it couldn't possibly fail because he had provided for every possible contingency, which he enumerated in exhaustive – and exhausting – detail. And while listening to all this, she said, her confidence in Flexner's martial prowess was at war with her fear for his safety. "I don't blame you," Flexner said; "That man was the most formidable enemy I ever went up against."

Flexner stopped talking for a while. Then Prudence said, "I overheard what he said to you. Do you think he was playing games with your mind?"

"He was trying to, that's for certain."

"And when you dropped your sword and said, come get me, were you trying to play with *his* mind – to make him overconfident, or something?"

"I sure hoped to God that would work."

"Thank God it did," Prudence breathed.

"Thank God is right. If it hadn't been for the storm, and a lot of lucky breaks, we wouldn't be on this horse."

"I love you," she said very quietly, but what with all his pain and his struggling to keep himself upright in the saddle, she wasn't sure he heard her.

When they arrived back at Fortress Andrew, Prudence secured as much help as she needed to get Flexner down from Ares, and get him put to bed. She arranged to have the Bonesetter called for that night, and a special cot provided for her in their quarters, so she could sleep in the same room with the patient without disturbing him. She wrote down the gist of what happened and gave the scroll to a courier, to take immediately to the Castle Royal and personally put into Her Majesty's hands, and she secured some strong sleeping medicine – very high proof drinking alcohol – which she gave to Flexner when they were alone in their quarters. After he had taken a sip of it, he said, "did I remember to thank you for what you did for me tonight?"

"You don't need to," she said, "I love you. But did I remember to thank you for saving my life?"

"Unnecessary," he said. "Same reason."

FORTY-SEVEN

You're still my Queen.

"Her Majesty wants to see you immediately," said Prudence to Flexner the next morning. "But I'm wondering if we shouldn't just tell her that you're in too much pain – what with the Bonesetter's being here a few hours ago."

"It's not that, not that really," said Flexner, "it's that I'm so ... I smell like a pigsty. I don't know how you can stand me."

"I was going to wash you tomorrow," she said, "but I can do it right now if you'd like."

"I'd be grateful, if you wouldn't mind."

So Prudence gave orders that a large basin of very warm water be prepared, another basin with a mixture of warm water, wood ashes and animal fat, and a bundle of rags provided. Once these were delivered, she bade everyone leave her alone with her husband, whom she proceeded to give a sponge bath. Her procedure was to moisten a rag with the warm water, then dip the rag into the watery mixture of wood ashes and animal fat, and with the rag thus prepared, gently lave the skin. She started with the face, which she washed with great tenderness, and then worked her way down his massive body.

"I hate to see you slaving so hard over me," Flexner murmured, to which she replied, "I'm not slaving; I'm loving."

When she had made her way to his privates, her washing became exquisitely tender, and when she felt him stiffen in her hands, she thought, *he's not so badly off as I thought!* She gave his penis a proprietary look and wondered, *How am I supposed to accommodate all this?* She glanced at Lord John, but he had his eyes closed, and she thought: *At some point, he's going to have to open his eyes!*

In time, the washing was over, although Prudence wouldn't have minded it taking longer. Clean bedding was brought and laid out by the chambermaids, who were a gift from Anna as part of her dowry. And a fresh linen tunic was brought for Flexner to wear in bed. Normally, he went to bed naked – which Prudence found very exciting – but it was considered disrespectful for him to be undressed under the bedclothes when Her Majesty was visiting. The final step – combing his hair and beard – had to be hurried, since all had heard the Royal Heraldic Trumpets signaling that Her Majesty would arrive in a few moments.

Within minutes, a Royal Page announced the presence of Her Majesty. All bowed as Anna entered and went directly to Flexner's bed.

"I'm sorry I cannot rise to welcome you, Your Majesty," said Flexner.

"No, I'm the one who needs to apologize," said Anna, kneeling at his bedside.

"Should I leave you both alone?" Prudence said.

"No, no – you two are husband and wife," said Anna, "and what one may hear, so may the other – unless I've overstepped here." She looked inquiringly at Lord John.

He did not disappoint. "Your Majesty, you're right: As my wife and partner, My Lady may hear anything I hear."

"That's wonderful!" cried Anna, and she beamed at them both. Prudence smiled shyly, but Flexner wore an expression of studied neutrality. "And now said Anna, "here is why I've come: First, I need to thank you, My Lord, for finally getting rid of Vieuxtemps. I knew that if anyone could, you would, and now you *have*. For the people of Grandlandia, I thank you with all my heart." She took his good hand in both of hers, and said "Thank you, John," and he kissed the hands that were holding his.

Anna continued: "You have given our people the gift of being able to live normally – at least for a little while."

"A little while?"

"I'm getting to that. But first I need to apologize to you for my part in Vieuxtemps' attack on you."

Flexner was incredulous. "You had a part in this?"

"François tried to seduce me. And instead of telling him a flat *no,* I said that General Flexner would have a fit if he knew about it. And although Vieuxtemps wasn't in the room with us, he somehow sensed François's frustration, and decided to do what his master would want him to do – assassinate you."

There was a long silence.

Finally, Flexner spoke: "With all due respect, ma'am, may I ask why you didn't simply tell him *no?*"

Anna looked distinctly uncomfortable. "I'm still trying to figure that one out. It's complicated. I had persuaded myself that – since we could never get away with having François killed, the next best thing would be to have him fall in love with me so that he'd have a vested interest not only in keeping me alive, but also happy. But if I sent him away feeling bitter, I would be provoking invasion. All that seems true and above board, I think. What *isn't* above board, but deeply shameful, is *why* I suggested to him that I might yield to his desire *if it weren't for you,* John. The shameful truth is—"

"You don't have to go any further, Ma'am," Flexner interrupted.

"No, I want to, I *need* to," Anna said, verging on tears, "and I know that whatever we say here never leaves this room."

"Of course! Right, right!" chorused Flexner and Prudence.

"The shameful truth," continued Anna, "is that part of me ..." she searched for words ... "part of me ... *wasn't so opposed* to a dalliance with François; the other part of course was disgusted by it. He was able to get as far as he did because of his superficial resemblance to Andrew. Yes, I was ... I was ..." She trailed off.

"Attracted to him?" Prudence ventured.

Anna spoke very quietly. "Yes," she said, "I was. But I was also afraid of him, and even more afraid of myself. So I thought, as long as my Man-Mountain stands between me and my desire, I'm safe!"

"You nearly lost your man-mountain," Flexner said.

"I know it, I know it! Can you forgive me?"

"I already have," said Flexner. "You're human, like the rest of us. You may not be perfect, but you're the best we could ever hope for, and we're lucky to have you. You're still my Queen."

"And mine," said Prudence.

Anna was crying, and it took a while for her to gain self control. When she did, she rose and went to Prudence, took her hand and drew her to Flexner. She joined their hands. "You're lucky to have him," she said.

"Actually," said Flexner, "we're both lucky. I may not be quite the keenest wit in the class, but I'm smart enough to know my good luck when I find it." He smiled at Prudence, and she smiled back so tremulously that Anna said, "And *I* know when *I'm* not needed."

"No, no," Prudence said, "you're *always* needed, ma'am."

"Nonsense, my dears, I know better. Even a Queen can be one too many, as I have been more times than I'd care to admit. I just want you two to know that this evening, I'm going to tell François the flat *no* I should have said the first time. God knows what will happen." She turned to Prudence. "Lady Alder, I know you'll take good care of your Lord, and it's a relief to know he's in your loving hands. His country may need its General once again."

FORTY-EIGHT

Now the real work begins.

"Is Lord John going to be all right?" François asked. He was in Anna's private suite, late that evening.

"Yes, Lord John will recover, no thanks to you," said Anna. "Your creature, Vieuxtemps, followed your orders, and came within an inch of killing him."

"I didn't order it."

"But you *thought* it," Anna said, "and Vieuxtemps, reading your mind, tried to *do* it. Do you think that not actually speaking the order relieves you of the responsibility?"

"It's a good thing Vieuxtemps is dead," he said.

"So you're disowning him, are you, now he can no longer serve you?"

Anna was angry, her cheeks pink with fury, and to François she seemed more beautiful than ever. "Surely," he said, "you're not going to let this lamentable incident come between us? *Quel dommage!* "

"You try to kill one of our most loyal subjects, you try to destroy the pillar of our realm, and you call it a lamentable incident?"

"Blame my passion for you, cherie: When I heard of Flexner's opposition to our union, I went mad. You must know that you have that effect on men – they go crazy for you."

"So it's my fault, now?"

"You led me on! We kissed!"

"And I said then that kissing you was no better than kissing Andrew's picture, but how wrong I was – it's much worse! When I kiss Andrew's picture, I'm kissing not only his image but what was behind it – his generosity, his nobility, his courage. But when I kissed you, I was kissing ... I'm nauseous to think of it ... I was kissing ... *Vieuxtemps! Ugh!"*

"So, I disgust you, do I, Votre Majesté?

"Yes, I feel disgust - and pity. Because you'll go back to your country and no longer be able to hide behind Vieuxtemps. When you commit some horrible crime - for that's really your nature - you'll no longer be able to say, "look what my crazy courtier has done in my name. It's lamentable *sans doute,* but what can I do? He gets carried away!" All this she pronounced in an exaggerated French accent.

His laughter had a cutting edge. "*Merveilleux!* So this is how it ends - with *une grande tirade dramatique* in which she pronounces her own ... how do you say? Death Warrant."

"Why am I not surprised?" Anna said. "You are, in your own opinion, a great god who can say, *love me or else*. You say, *since you don't love me, you die!* Don't you understand, *Votre Majesté,* that there are people who would *rather* die than submit to such tyranny?"

"Très bien! You want to die? You will get your wish!"

"What - right now?" Anna's body tensed.

"What do you take me for - *un fou*? You probably have your people hidden all over the place! *Non!* I'm not such a fool - *non! We* will wait until *my* people reappear in a few weeks. Then, you'll see! THEN, not only you, but every last person in your pitiful country will die the death because ... BECAUSE ... **BECAUSE YOU DARED REJECT *FRANÇOIS DE BOURGOGNE - LE GRAND!"***

By the end of this tirade, François was fairly screaming. He slammed his fist on her council table so hard that the cherry wood casket with its precious contents jumped audibly.

Anna went toward the entrance of her suite, calling "Guards! GUARDS! Come here – I need you!"

Whereupon the four guards stationed at the entranceway ran in, swords drawn.

Anna was in full imperial mode. "Guards," she said, "this man here has just threatened to kill us. Seize him! Take him down to the cellar; lock him up in cell number 2 and keep him guarded every minute of the day and night. And if he gives any trouble, let us know, so we can decide whether to kill him now, or later." Whereupon the guards seized the stunned François the Great and dragged him away.

With François gone, Anna sat down, exhausted. She said out loud, to no one in particular: "Now the real work begins."

FORTY-NINE

Give me a kiss, poor wifey.

The Lord and Lady of Pleasantvale (Turco and Angelina) were awakened from sleep by a loud banging on the door. Turco got out of bed, threw on a robe, grabbed his sword, and went to the door. He opened it to find a royal courier who said, “Her Majesty requests that you attend her *immediately*, and have her be awakened should she be asleep.” The courier placed in Turco’s hand a scroll with the same information.

Turco said to him, “Please tell Her Majesty that I am leaving as soon as I can get some clothes on and kiss my wife goodbye. Go ahead now, *fly,* and I’ll be following soon after.”

Angelina was agitated. “What’s going on,” she said, “that would make Her Majesty wake us up in the middle of the night to ask you to attend her *immediately,* even to wake her if she’s sleeping? Could she be ill?”

“It’s always possible,” said Turco, “but I tend to doubt it. If she were ill, she might have trouble sleeping. Whatever it is, we’ll know within an hour or so.”

“You mean, *you’ll* know. Poor wifey here will have to wait patiently until she hears the news along with everyone else.”

Within five minutes, Turco was dressed and ready to go. “Give me a kiss, poor wifey,” he said; “your poor husband wishes he were in bed with you.”

After the kiss, he was out the door, and onto his horse.

Angelina mused, *this is what it is to be married to a great man.*

FIFTY

That Tends to Simplify Things.

Later that day, Princess Jane came into the Council Room. Anna the Queen scarcely looked up. "What's the matter, are you pregnant?"

"Is that a way for you to greet your only sister?"

"Since I granted you daily visits from Emanuel," said Anna, "you've scarcely bothered to visit *your* only sister, being too busy, I suppose, with *him* to pay any attention to *me.*"

"Well, I'm sorry about that and I'll try to do better. And *you* can be nicer to me."

Anna heaved a deep sigh and regarded Jane seriously – for the first time, it seemed to them both, in days. "We can begin," she said, by your answering my question: Are you pregnant?"

"No!" cried Jane, "and that's the problem: I've been trying everything I could think of to seduce him, but he insists that he wants to begin our marriage on a solid footing, and that means doing things right and waiting 'til our wedding night."

"I see," said Anna. "The apple sure fell far from *that* tree."

"Yes it did."

"And now you're frustrated."

"Well not exactly. I mean we're together, and we kiss and we ... well, you get the idea: It can be very satisfying."

"Then what are you complaining about?" said Anna, who got up and walked a little away from her sister. "You are a very lucky woman, Jane," she said, not looking at her.

Jane rose, too. "Oh God!" she cried, "I know I sound spoiled and selfish, and I maybe I am, because I've forgotten just how lucky I am, compared to you. Your situation is horrible, but should every woman in the realm forswear happiness because *you* have?"

They stood like that for what seemed a long time, with Anna's back to her sister, until Anna finally turned to Jane. "All right. What do you want me to do?" she said.

"I want you to let us get married."

"There will be a howl from the Lords."

"Let them howl. From what I understand, you've just thrown King François into a dungeon. That may well mean death for all of us when his ships come back for him. The Lords should worry less about appearances and more about saving the nation. And if the truth be known, Emanuel is twice the man of any of those Lords, and if they don't know it, I'll tell 'em!"

Anna smiled. "That's my girl – you tell 'em."

"Now how are we going to manage it?" Jane said.

"We?" Anna smiled, but forebore saying, "what do you mean, *we?"* Instead she said, "If François is content to go back to France without invading us, then we'll have a grand public wedding in the Cathedral. If we go to war, well – we'll have to get Friar Anselm up here to marry you privately, and postpone the public part. So your virtuous fiancé should be content with the legality of things, and should be willing to treat you like a proper husband. Any more questions?"

"Yes, one: How do you manage to do it all, Anna?"

"I don't have a choice. That tends to simplify things."

FIFTY-ONE

It's your gruesome, waking truth!

François' first day in the dungeon wasn't a full day at all, for he was imprisoned at about 10 p.m. When he saw that the place was windowless, and was lit only by 6 candles, he said: "Is this all the light there is? Isn't there a window, somewhere?"

His Chief Jailer looked at him as if he were crazy.

François started to mumble, "she'll pay. She'll pay."

"What's that, My Lord?" said his jailer.

"Not that it's any of your business, but I said that Queen Anna will pay for having thrown an anointed King into this dark hole."

"I don't know nothin' 'bout that stuff," said the Jailer. All I know is that if ye say or do somethin' causin' a problem, we're to report it to her Majesty right away. So if I were ye – and thank God I'm not – I'd watch what I say in 'ere – though if ye really did threaten Her Majesty, yer goose may be cooked *already.* Threatening the Queen is serious business."

"So is throwing an honored guest into a place like this! My people will hear of it!"

"Yer people ain't exactly here right now, are they, milord? But *our* people are!"

And with that, François was unceremoniously thrust into a cell which had nothing but a straw pallet and a toilet basin.

At midnight, four candles were extinguished, leaving two candles lit. "Jailer!" François called, "can you make it just a *little* brighter in here?". "I'm not used to the dark – it's unlucky."

"I don't know about unlucky. Ye give people some time down here, they get used ter the dark. They become regular moles."

"There's nothing I would find more repugnant."

"Well then, ye're in the right place," said the Jailer. "Ye weren't sent down here to be *entertained,* now were ye?"

François took this in, and then instead of a rejoinder, decided to say, simply, "Good night, Jailer."

"Good night, Frenchy."

His second day began and proceeded uneventfully except for the fact that his meals were not only brought punctually, but they showed that someone was taking great care with his food – not only in quantity, but in quality. Fresh fruits and baked goods still warm from the oven were not the usual fare for prisoners, he felt sure. Most of all, the kindling of four additional candles made the daytime less unbearable.

Bringing in his breakfast on a glistening round tray, the jailer remarked, "Her Majesty can't be *too* mad at ye. I can tell by the likes of this breakfast that she means to keep ye around for a while."

"Thanks for bringing this promptly," said François, "the bread is still warm."

"Only followin' orders."

With such chit-chat at meal times, François tried to alleviate the loneliness of his imprisonment. The Jailer, for his part, was happy to have someone to talk to – probably for the same reason: Solitary confinement is itself a torture, and apparently Her Majesty had not forbidden this human contact – such as it was.

But at midnight, things darkened – visibly at first, when four of the six candle flames were extinguished. Instead of complaining, François lay down hoping to get the sleep he was unable to get the evening before. It wasn't too long before his deep breathing showed that blessed slumber finally was visiting him.

It wasn't a long visit. A kind of creaking woke him, and he sat bolt upright: That sound seemed to be right inside his cell! His eyes stabbed the darkness, and he thought he saw at the side of his pallet a ... *shape*, dark and formless and tilting back and forth ever so slightly, ever so slowly, as if it were almost alive.

It seemed to groan his name: "François ... François ..."

Am I dreaming – of a shape? *Just* ... a shape? *Bad omen!* "What are you?" he managed.

"I am what's left of Vieuxtemps," it said, with a voice that was also a moan, "and I am returned to bring you a warning ... a warning ..."

"About what?"

With a dismal groan, the shape continued: "I warn you: Go back to France, and never come back ... don't even think of it ..."

"Why not? Why shouldn't I?" François' voice quavered.

"Do you know how it feels to be strangled?" the shape moaned, "it's horrible, *horrible!* You gag on your own spit as you choke into the dark ... that's what you did to me ..."

"*I* did?!"

"Yes," it groaned, "when you wrote to Queen Anna, 'Do what you must to get rid of Vieuxtemps.' You betrayed me, François – *we were so close!* But you cast me off to where there is no light, *no air to breathe!* You will know what it is when you join me some day, which you surely will, sooner or later. But should you even *think* about returning from France, or even *think* to send men in your place, you will see me sooner, so much sooner ..."

"I'm not afraid of you – I'll wake up soon; this is only a dream!"

"Don't you wish it were!" cried the shape, which emitted a hideous, cackling laugh. "You'll never wake up from *this* nightmare; it's your gruesome, waking truth!" And with hideous laughter, the shape sank into the ground while François fell back on the bed, his flesh crawling. Sleep did not visit him again that night.

The next day went about the same as the prior one, except that each time the jailer appeared, François debated with himself as to whether he should confide to the Jailer what had happened. Each time he decided against it: What he had heard and seen might have been the products of his feverish imagination, and he didn't want the jailer to think him crazy.

The four candles were extinguished on schedule, and François, already exhausted from the prior sleepless night, resolved to get some sleep. But an hour later he awoke to feel on his shoulder five hawk-like talons piercing his flesh. His eyes opened to be filled with the sight of a green-faced figure holding aloft a lantern with a single candle in it. "François, François," it wailed, "your man, Vieuxtemps, gave me no choice, no way out! Instead he gave me a crossbow to shoot at Her Majesty! And if I refused, he would strangle my wife and three kids in front of my eyes! I knew he could do it, I'd *seen* him do it to others, with their hands tied behind their backs, and a garrot wire tightening around their necks, cutting deep into their necks – there was no way out for *them!*" The figure covered his face with his hand. "Oh God," he wailed from behind his hand, "what could I do? I aimed that cross-bow, I aimed it – but at the last moment, thank God, I raised my aim and shot that bolt over the Queen's carriage, so Her Majesty could live! Which meant that I would have to die by Hemlock poison, or see my wife and little ones strangled. So I went home, told the kids to go out and play, and asked my wife to bring me some porridge." From the folds of his cloak the figure produced a square bowl. "She brought the porridge in a square-shaped bowl *just like this*; the porridge smelled delicious. I mixed into it the Hemlock powder that *your man* Vieuxtemps had given me, and then I ate it. All of it. Aargh! Don't let anyone tell you that death by Hemlock is painless, oh no: I retched, I vomited, I shook until I could no longer stand, and then I lay down and lost sensation first in my toes, then in my feet, my shins, my thighs, and so on upward, and through it all I was completely clear in my mind. Over and over I told my wife how much I loved her, I could hear her say the same, over and over, and she held my hand until, when I could no longer breathe, my light ... went out."

The figure blew out the candle in his lantern, and in the darkness said, "François, *your man* did all this to me, all this and more to many others, whose widows and children still are wailing. If you listen carefully, you can hear them!" And faintly, dimly in the darkness came the cries of women and children, surmounted by the soft voice of the figure saying, "If I were you, François, I'd be afraid to sleep for fear you'll dream of sending other men to do your bidding over here. For if you even dream of such a thing, ***you may learn what it is to be served THE SQUARE-SHAPED BOWL. You'll have no way out."***

The next morning the Jailor cheerily brought François his breakfast tray, which held a sliced melon, toasted pastries still warm, and piping hot porridge – *in a square-shaped bowl.* The prisoner looked at it and gagged, retched, and vomited.

"Uh-oh," cried the Jailor, "they said you might be sick, and to send word if you did."

The next thing François knew was that he was in the guest bed in which he had originally lain down when he arrived in Grandlandia. Someone had put him in fresh night clothes; someone had washed him clean. The only trace of his ordeal in the cellar was the foul taste in his mouth, and a tormenting headache. Standing at his bedside, wiping his forehead with a damp cloth, was Her Majesty. "Oh, you've opened your eyes," she said, "that's a good sign, *Votre Majesté.* Some prisoners have a very severe reaction to imprisonment down there; they get really sick, and that may have happened to you, or it could have been that you were coming down with something even before you were sent down there – you really were violent!

But we don't want you to be sick – we want you to get better, so we can send you back to France in health. We want your people to look at your face and see that we Grandlandians love people who visit us in peace." She pointed to a kindly looking lady in late middle-age.

"François," Anna said, "I want you to meet Iolanta here, who is to do everything needed to help you recover from your sickness." She pointed to two burly armed guards. "And over there are Isdreth and Anguk, who'll make sure to remind you – in case you forget – that you must never leave your guest room. When it comes time for you to depart – which will be in a week – Isdreth and Anguk will be among your many friends wishing you *bon voyage*. There's no need for you to reply. Just relax and get your strength back." And with that, Anna blew François a kiss, and left the room.

FIFTY-TWO

Wake up.

The week passed in a haze of bonhomie. François, now strong enough to sit up in a chair, received many visits of well-wishing Grandlandians, some expressing their felicitations in carefully rehearsed French. When the day came, Anna's Ladies in Waiting came to help him dress in his finest clothes, which had been well washed during the week.

Carefully attended by Isdreth and Anguk, now enjoying the temporary sobriquet of "Honor Guards," François appeared before Anna herself, to bid farewell. He bowed before her and said, *"Votre Majesté,* you are a very beautiful woman."

"And *you* are still dreaming. Wake up."

"I am fully awake, *Majesté,* and I tell you that not only you're a very beautiful woman, but the smartest woman it has been my honor to know."

"Smart? Hah! Maybe on sunny days, when the clouds are purple. As for most days, you should know better than anyone else that I'm far from infallible."

"That shall be our secret, *Majesté;* no one will hear it from MY lips."

"Nor from mine, François. I see you've woken up and I'm glad of it. But are *you* glad you're awake?"

"There are things that happened between us that make me wish I were dreaming again. But there are other things – like those nightmares – I wouldn't go through those again for all the world.

"Votre Majesté," she said, "no one can force you to relive those nightmares if you don't want to. That's an advantage of being *Roi* – you can live the life you want, not the life you're told to live. I wish you a life of good health, sunny days and happy dreams."

"And I wish the same to you, *Majesté."*

He bowed, she nodded in return, and he took his leave – accompanied by Isdreth and Anguk, his "Honor Guards" – passing downstairs through the inner and outer courtyards along both sides of which stood the castle servants, all applauding. Before he climbed into his coach, a little girl ran up to him with a bouquet of wildflowers.

"A posy for you, sir," she said.

"Oh! Thank you *ma petite,* he said. "I love posies – I arrived here with one. May I kiss your hand?"

"Yes sir," she said shyly. She held her hand up higher than her head, to make it easier for him.

And so *le Roi François de Bourgogne Le Grand* bowed low and delicately kissed the proffered hand, then he straightened, and she curtsied, evoking another round of applause.

François, together with his guards, got into the carriage and set out on the road to Middleburgh, the port town at which he first set foot in Grandlandia. On the way, he encountered hundreds of men, women and children who had come out to cheer him. He waved to them happily.

Once arrived in Middleburgh, and having emerged from his carriage, François went up to the leader of his escort, Count Edgar of Ravenshead, and said to him, "*Monsieur le Comte*, please convey to General Flexner my thanks for protecting me while I was here, and my hopes that he will heal very soon."

"I will sir," said Edgar, bowing smartly.

And so *François de Bourgogne* stepped into the sixteen-oared long boat commanded by Sir Hubert Brookford. His departure had been marked by sweetness, light, and flowers, but as the crew rowed toward the French flotilla waiting on the horizon, François could not help but see on the beaches the thousands of men with cross bows, long bows with flame tipped arrows, with spears, swords and shields - all intended to deter a French landing. François waved to them gaily, and they – with appropriate sobriety – waved back.

FIFTY-THREE

I refuse to live fearing the worst.

It was a good omen. After François had finally climbed up onto his 120-oar bireme, he ordered its captain to head back to France. Horns were blown; the bireme set off for home; and the rest of the fleet followed. Sir Hubert waited until all the ships had disappeared over his horizon, then, figuring there was nothing more he could do, instructed his 16 oarsmen to head back to shore.

By that time, of course, in Anna's council room there was general rejoicing. General John Flexner chose this moment to emerge from convalescence in Fortress Andrew – despite the heated objections of his Bonesetter, who had put on him a cast stiffened with egg white, flour, and animal fat, and who had predicted dire consequences if Flexner moved about before six more weeks had elapsed. Therefore Lady Prudence insisted on coming with her husband, and – despite his barely concealed annoyance – hovered over him like a mother hen.

Anna the Queen wasted no time in lavishing praise upon her General, whom she termed the country's savior, calling his heroism more than equal to Grandlandia's emergency. Flexner, however, said that he was the beneficiary of stupendous God-given luck, and that – as soon as his cast was off – he intended to give thanks to the Lord in the Great Cathedral.

"Yes, of course," Anna acknowledged, "the Lord is to thank for all of this, but I think we can all agree that in our General the Lord has had an instrument perfect for

His purpose!" This pronouncement elicited grumpy frowns from Flexner, and general applause from everyone else – especially from Lady Prudence.

"Yes," said Turco, "without General Flexner we would have been in dire straits indeed. But let's not forget the genius of Her Majesty, whose adroit tactics turned what could have been a national disaster into a national triumph!"

"Genius?" said Anna, "I highly doubt it, Lord Turco. It was more like lucky blundering on my part that let things turn out the way they did. But if you want to talk about genius, don't forget your dazzling acting, without which our ruse would have fallen flat."

"Well," said Turco, "all the background information given me by General Flexner, not to mention everyone's helpful suggestions – especially Lady Prudence's brilliant idea about the square shaped bowl – all of that really helped pull it off. And that Chorus of Innocents – all those grieving women and children – they were so realistic! They brought out my best efforts."

Anna spoke up: "Hannah Moro – the handmaid to the Princess – played the martyr's wife, and rehearsed the chorus. I'll make sure to thank her personally."

"What about that trap door in Cell 2?" asked Count Edgar. "It seemed designed exactly for this purpose!"

"It wasn't though, quite obviously," said Anna. "That feature was installed by Queen Thanata. It connects by a passageway to another barred entrance in a little known cell. To this barred entrance only she had the key, and she secretly used it to rescue condemned prisoners whom she favored, and secretly to murder others whom *the populace* generally favored. I found the key. It was labeled and I learned its function. That's what gave me the idea."

"Not that I want to say anything good about Thanata," said Count Edgar. "The stench of her evil lingers even today. But perhaps it is a mistake to claim that the late Queen was *completely* bad, since in providing a trap door and secret passageway, Thanata had done one good thing."

But she used it for unworthy purposes," said Turco, and it remained for her successor, our noble Queen, to use it for good. In my opinion, therefore, the trap door redounds to the credit only of Her Majesty, and not one bit to Thanata."

"So say we all!" shouted General Flexner, evoking applause and hurrahs all around.

At that moment, one of the Castle guards entered and said, "Your Majesty, Her Royal Highness is outside, and begs admittance."

"To disturb our council?" asked Edgar.

"Our council has devolved into a celebration," said Anna, "and I see no reason why we should exclude Princess Jane. She is my sister."

So Jane was admitted, and she went directly to Anna and whispered something in her ear.

"Really!" Anna exclaimed. She turned to Turco. "Lord Turco, Her Royal Highness has informed me that Lady Angelina is with child. This is striking news; why didn't you tell us?"

"I didn't want to trouble your Majesty with it," said Turco.

"It's no trouble; I'm sure all of us here pray for a safe delivery – healthy baby and healthy mother."

"Amen," everyone murmured.

Anna turned to Jane. “Thank you for your news, Jane. Is there anything else you want to tell us?”

“Yes: I envy Lady Angelina. No wait - don’t say anything - I know this is a delicate and dangerous time for her, and I know that she may die - God forbid. And yet I wish I were in her position. I have a fiancé whom I love unspeakably and whom I wish to treasure with the greatest gift I can give him - a child. If that meant dying for him, I would do it - gladly.”

There was a brief silence, then Edgar asked, “Who is this lucky man?”

“His name,” said Anna, “is Emanuel Agright, Viscount of Domeny.”

Another silence, which took all of four or five seconds, but which felt to Jane like as many years.

Anna the Queen continued: “He comes from good family, despite the blot that was his father, and he is perfect for Jane - *perfect.* They love each other deeply. She will consider no one else, and neither will I. *I want this to happen.”*

Jane gave Anna a look of passionate gratitude.

“Well,” said Turco, “if you want it, then so do I.”

“So do I,” said Edgar.

“And I too,” said Flexner.

“Then this is how we’ll plan it: Lord Turco, when is your darling wife due to deliver?”

“In six or seven weeks, so please your Majesty.”

“So far along, is she! Had she favored us with a visit, we would have known her condition long before now.”

“It is my fault,” Turco, said, “I felt it better for her to be at home. Please forgive me.”

"My dear Lord, we're in the mood to forgive you everything! "So here's what we'll do: when it comes time for the baby to be baptized, we'll use the occasion also to celebrate the marriage of Her Royal Highness and Lord Agright, and at the same time, we'll have a special service to thank God for saving Grandlandia through the efforts – not only of our hero, General Flexner, but the efforts of *everyone.*"

"It all sounds so wonderful," said Jane, "but what if ... God forbid ... what if ...?"

"We'll hear no what-ifs, Princess Jane," said Anna, "We'll proceed as if God will continue to bless us. Sure, there is always the possibility of ... something else. And if we have to face that, we will. But I refuse to live fearing the worst. I'll hope for the best, and live by that. Are there objections to this?

There were not.

FIFTY-FOUR

When we ALL are stronger

Raised on a temporary platform within the Grand Cathedral stood Queen Anna herself, flanked by General Flexner (his arm still in his cast) and Count Edgar of Ravenshead. On the ground before them stood much of Grandlandia's landed aristocracy. Positioned in the aisles were some of the nation's crack troops, heavily armed. The point was lost on no one: What Her Majesty was about to pronounce would be backed up, if necessary, by all the force at her command – which by now was formidable.

She spoke: "My Lords and Ladies of Grandlandia, we are pleased and proud to announce that a serious threat to our realm has been averted, thanks to our stalwart Lord General John Flexner of Nightwood. Our Man-Mountain is a bulwark to us all, and we salute him!"

An ovation erupted, and Anna joined in the applause herself, turning, as she applauded, to face Lord John who looked both pleased yet uncomfortable. When the applause died away, Anna continued: "Because of this threat, Lords and Ladies, we couldn't address a problem which concerns us all. But now that the threat has been averted, we can turn the full force of our attention to resolving this issue. That is why we've called you here.

"Not too many years have elapsed since our coronation in this very cathedral, where most of you saw the Priests put on our finger the ring that symbolizes our marriage to the nation. Look: We're still wearing it. And they gave us a Holy Bible and told us: 'Here is Wisdom.

This is the Royal Law; these are the lively oracles of God.' Well, Lords and Ladies, now that the insurrection has been put down, we've had time to read this Bible – and we *have* read it, cover to cover. We've learned a lot. And one of the things we've learned is that we have a duty not only to all you Lords and Ladies, but to *everyone* – even to the lowliest person in our realm. You all have a duty to protect *us,* and we, in turn, have a duty to protect you – *all* of you. Thus your serfs and your tenants are not yours only – they're also *ours.* So when you abuse them, you're abusing *us.* I say *when* you abuse them, because I've seen how wretched are the lives of some of the lowest among you, whose helpless vulnerability you exploit for your own profit.

Anna the Queen took a step forward on the platform. "*This must stop*", she declared. "We, as Queen, have a sacred duty to make sure it stops." There was a murmuring in her audience, but Anna raised her voice and spoke over it: ***"Listen to us:*** You, as our subjects, have just as sacred a duty to *help* us make it stop."

Now there was absolute silence. Anna continued, her voice ringing: "Thanks to the blessing of God," she said, "and to the great efforts of many of you, peace has been restored to our realm. But peace *will not last* if some among us are oppressed simply because they have the misfortune of being born to the wrong parents. Now we know we cannot legislate morality. What we *can* do, however, is send out among you our agents to gauge your progress in ensuring loving justice to the lowest among you. If any of you fails to make progress in this, we shall learn of it and take corrective measures. Some of these corrections may not be pleasant. But we are firmly convinced that our nation will be stronger not merely when some of us are stronger, but when we *all* are stronger."

The applause started politely, but then it gathered strength and enthusiasm, giving Anna the hope that her speech, which took her hours to craft, had touched *some*body.

FIFTY-FIVE
The Birth

I've just had another contraction," Lady Angelina said to her husband, Lord Turco.

"What do you mean, *another?* Have they started? Why didn't you tell me?"

"Because I need you more than ever, and I was afraid to be hidden away in a dark room alone."

"But you won't be alone, darling. Mistress Ridgely, the midwife, will attend you. She's attended many of the highest-born ladies in Grandlandia, and she comes very well recommended. And not only will she be there, but Her Royal Highness Princess Jane insists on being there to help also, and she wants to bring her handmaid, Hannah Moro."

"All that's fine, but it isn't enough. *I want you to be with me.*"

"And I want to be with you, too, my darling, but I'm afraid to be seen there."

"Why?" Angelina demanded, a trifle querulously. "Are you afraid to soil your hands with it? That's what they all think – that childbirth is women's business, filthy, unfit for men even to see, let alone soil themselves with."

"Of course I don't think that way, Angelina – I hope you know me better than that. I think that idea is stupid – barbaric, really. Giving birth is a blessing – a beautiful thing. But my being there would create such a scandal that I'm afraid Mistress Ridgley would quit. And then where would we be?"

"Well, darling, couldn't *you* deliver the baby?" She asked this in all innocence.

"I wish I could, my love, but I don't think I can help deliver babies. For that we need a midwife. Don't worry – I won't leave the house the way most husbands would. I'll be right here if you need me. But you're not going to need me; you're going to be just fine."

But she wasn't just fine. After her waters broke, her screams penetrated to every corner of the house while Turco, two rooms away, sat motionless, beads of sweat on his forehead. But as the hours went by, the screams grew weaker, and finally stopped. A panicked Jane came to him in his study. "My Lord," she said, "Lady Angelina's in trouble. Her labor has stopped, and Mistress Ridgley says she can't do much to help."

"I'm going in there."

"Mistress Ridgely says that if you come in, she'll leave."

"Will she then? Listen: As soon as I get in there, I want you and Goody Moro to block the door; don't let her out. Only the midwife can deliver Angelina."

Turco's bursting into the room, and Mistress Ridgely's "I'm leaving!" came in quick succession, and Jane's and Moro's blocking her exit followed soon thereafter. Turco confronted the midwife. "What's going on here?" he said.

"Her labor has stopped, and there's not much I can do," said the midwife. "I fear the outcome."

Angelina lay on the bed, a ghastly pallor on her face.

"Why is she lying down?" said Turco.

"That's how the ladies of quality give birth around here," said the midwife, a short, round and muscular little woman.

"What about a birthing stool?"

"I tried it, and Milady doesn't like it."

"But you can see her current position's not working." Turco took a moment to think. "Hm ... look: I have an idea, but I need your help, Mistress Ridgley; will you help me?"

The midwife looked non-plussed. "I have never heard of such a thing in my whole life!" she cried. "What will people say?"

"Who cares? Do you want to save this woman's life, or don't you?"

Mistress Ridgley's professional ethic couldn't resist that question. "What do you want from me?" she said.

"Help me get her out of bed – *gently*. We want her standing; I'll stand behind her, supporting her with my arms under her armpits, so she can be in a semi-squat position without having to use any strength to hold herself up. And then the force of gravity will help us."

"Gravity?"

"It's in Aristotle, but don't worry about it. Just help me please, and I think it might actually work."

The Midwife went to the bed, saying, "my professional career is over."

"We won't tell anyone – unless you want us to."

So Turco, with the assistance not only of Mistress Ridgley, but also of Jane and Hannah, very gently lifted Angelina out of bed, and with Turco's support, positioned her in a standing, semi-squat position, with her legs as far apart as was comfortable for her – some ten degrees wider than would have been possible in bed.

Turco placed his lips close to his Lady's ear. "Good girl," he softly said to her.

"Turco! You're here," she murmured. "Thank God!"

"I wouldn't miss it for the world," he said.

"Could I have some water, please?" Angelina said with a little more force.

Hearing that, Hannah left the room before Turco had a chance to ask her, and quickly returned with a cup of water which she held up to Angelina's lips. After a couple of sips, Angelina emitted a great cry, for the contractions had resumed.

"Good job!" cried Turco.

"Wonderful, My Lady!" said Jane.

And so the contractions resumed with increasing force, but because of Angelina's semi-squat position, each contraction was more productive and less painful than it otherwise would have been. Sensing all this, Angelina felt even stronger urges to push.

"Don't drop me!" Angelina told Turco.

"Don't worry, I'd rather die," he replied, and he said to Jane and Hannah, "if you see me weakening, support my arms and help me support her. And as for you, Mistress Ridgely, you position yourself underneath Angelina, and do what you know."

"You don't have to tell me," the midwife said with some asperity.

During the next hour and a half, there were a few occasions where Jane and Hannah did have to come to Turco's aid, but not many. And then Mistress Ridgely cried, "I see the head – your baby's hair is black!"

At this point the midwife took over – telling Angelina when to push, when not to push, and when to redouble pushing. In between these instructions, Turco, Jane, and Hannah took turns praising Angelina for the wonderful job she was doing.

"The head is out – most of the work is done!" cried the midwife, and it wasn't long before she held up a robust, heartily squalling baby boy to show his adoring parents.

Somehow, they got Angelina back into bed – Turco, Jane and Hannah assisting Angelina, with Mistress Ridgely holding the baby, who in due time, was placed in his mother's arms.

"You're my hero," said Turco to Angelina, "and you're mine," she said, and they kissed.

Then she murmured, "and you said that you couldn't help deliver babies."

"All right," he said, "I did help a little. But you did all the work!"

"Have you forgotten how hard you worked just to hold me up?"

"That wasn't work. I love you."

The midwife approached the bed and interrupted this idyll.

"Congratulations, My Lady; you did very well. Your baby looks beautiful – perfect. Good luck with him. You have good caretakers here. My job is over."

"Wait a minute," Turco said, I need to get something for you." And he left the room and returned with a bag full of coins.

Mistress Ridgely hefted the bag, and then opened it and looked in. "This looks like much more than we had agreed on, My Lord," she said.

"It is," said Turco, because I couldn't be more pleased, and also because I want you to keep this afternoon's activities secret. Nobody need know about it."

"And nobody will," she said; "I value my reputation."

"And you can use our new technique, if you like – and you can say it's yours."

"I'd love to try it again," she said, "but I don't know where I'd find another father as fearless as you – or as strong."

"It would be next to impossible," said Lady Angelina. "I've never met anyone who even comes close to my husband."

"Nor have I met anyone who even remotely approaches Angelina," Turco said in his turn, leaning in for another kiss. Then he turned to the midwife. "Please do have a pleasant evening, Mistress Ridgely. If you need a recommendation, we'll be glad to supply it."

Bowing gratefully, midwife showed herself out.

Angelina turned to Jane. "Your Royal Highness," she said, "I can't thank you enough for your help today – your help and Hannah's."

"What?" cried Jane, "do you think you can get rid of us so easily?"

"You're not going?"

"Not until you and your baby are strong enough to get him baptized. Hannah and I are going to stay here and care for each of you until you're both ready for the ceremony."

"Oh!" cried Angelina, "that's so generous of you!"

"Maybe. But I have a couple of selfish motives. First, I'd love to do a drawing or two of you nursing your little one – I've never drawn the Madonna, and you're a perfect subject for it."

"I'll be happy to serve. But you said you had a *couple* of selfish motives," said Angelina. "What's the other?"

"On the day that your baby is baptized, Her Majesty intends to see me married to Lord Emanuel Agright. So you might say that I have a vested interest in seeing you and your little one well and happy. I hope all that doesn't compromise my generosity."

"Not in the slightest," said Turco. "It makes it all the more sincere. Behind any generous deed, anybody can find selfish motives. So what? Just so long as you *do* the good deed, it makes little difference why you did it. I want you to take as much credit as you like, and Angelina and I will add plenty more – you deserve it!"

FIFTY-SIX

It has to happen!

Now that the danger from Vieuxtemps was over, and Flexner was out of his cast, it was appropriate that he and Lady Prudence move back to Flexner's grand mansion. They departed Fortress Andrew with great fanfare, with formal salutations and good wishes. Flexner commended the men's flawless discipline and great helpfulness during their stay there, and Lady Prudence, in her turn, thanked the men for helping her feel "as much at home as was possible under the circumstances." This was followed by volleys of huzzahs from the men, who doubtless were looking forward - if not to the absence of their Commander and his Bride - at least to the greater ease that their absence would make possible.

Their reception by the staff at Flexner's mansion was equally heartfelt, if not quite so voluble. The staff lined up in order of the size of their responsibilities, from the Porters to the Household Chamberlain; each bowed or curtsied murmuring *welcome home, Milord, Milady.* These murmured welcomes meant as much to them as all the huzzahs they had recently heard.

Knowing their Lord's and Lady's favorite dishes, the staff had prepared for them both a supper they knew would please - the couple's favorite - roast lamb and apples. The happy couple lingered over the wine and the dessert - apple pie with figs, raisins, and spices, and they made two toasts. The first he proposed: *To her Majesty's long life and health.* The second was Prudence's idea, which she offered hesitantly: "Do you think we should raise our glasses to: *our marriage – to its length and health?"*

"What do you mean *health?"* he asked. "Do you mean that we both should remain healthy?"

"Well yes, that of course, but also, that we continue to ... get along with each other?"

He thought a moment, and then ventured, "Yes, that makes perfect sense, because ..." he paused, then declared, "because if we get along with each other, the more likely we'll continue to be healthy – don't you think?"

"Oh yes, absolutely!" she said, her eyes sparkling.

Soon they were in their own bedroom. They sat next to each other on the bed. Flexner asked. "Do you feel ready for sleep?"

"Surely," she said, and began to unfasten a button – but then stopped. "Lady Angelina gave birth to a baby boy today," she said.

"Yes I know."

"They're calling him *Turco,* after the father."

"It's appropriate," he said; "it's more than that, actually. After his father's role in saving us from attack by the French, Turco's name ought to be held high in honor, and will be, if I have anything to say about it."

"It's wonderful to hear you speak that way," she said, "because you were not always on the best of terms with him."

"Well at my age, I hope I'm still capable of learning something," he said, looking at the floor. "This whole thing ..." He paused, and then went on: "This whole thing ... has made me ask myself ... well ... why was I so persistent about Her Majesty? I *knew* there was no future for me and her ... I mean *in that way.* I knew it. She would never need me *in that way.* She needed me to defend her throne, but that was it. I knew that. Everyone knew it. But why couldn't I really take it in?"

She placed her hand on his. "You're being too hard on yourself."

"I could see only *her* ... which made me unable to see anything else ... or any*one.*" He looked at her steadfastly. "I'm really sorry for ... for not seeing."

She drew his head toward her and she kissed him warmly. For a moment his eyes widened in surprise, then they closed as he returned her kiss, tentatively at first, and then with increasing ardor, wrapping his arms around her, learning as he went.

After a few minutes of this, he drew back and looked at her shyly. "I hope I'm doing this the right way," he said.

"Oh darling, you're wonderful ... *wonderful!*" she said, and threw herself into his arms, where they continued catching up to where they ought to have been when they married.

They broke again, laughing with the joy of relief and discovery. "My love," she breathed, "I was beginning to fear that this would never happen."

Again he looked away, and said in a low voice, "Well, on that night in Agright's old house where we saved each other's lives, I started thinking about how lucky we both were to be alive – and how lucky *I* was ..." he turned to face her and continued "... how lucky I was to have *you.* And then recently when Her Royal Highness burst in to the council room and said that she envied Lady Angelina's pregnancy, and that while she knew that giving birth is a dangerous business, she too wanted to bestow – no, that wasn't her word – she wanted to ... to *treasure* her fiancé—"

"Yes, *treasure,*" Prudence interrupted, "that was it ... *treasure* ..."

"Right. She wanted to *treasure* her fiancé with a child, and if that meant having to die, she'd gladly do it."

"I've heard some other women say that," said Prudence, "and I wondered, if I were deeply in love with a man, would I feel the same way?"

He looked at her. "And ...?"

She smiled. "The answer is, yes I would. And I *do.*"

He took both her hands and kissed them. "I feel I don't deserve such love," he said, and I feel I can't expect you to risk your life in bearing a child of mine—"

"No, no" she interrupted, "don't feel that way—"

"Please, sweetheart, let me finish. I was going to say that other women bearing children face too much risk as it is, but you – bearing mine – with my huge size and all – your risk might be double theirs, and I can't ask it."

"But I *want* it, don't you see? And where is it written that a child *has* to take after the father? It could take after the mother. Besides, do you have brothers and sisters?"

"Five of them."

"And are they all huge?"

"No – I'm the only one. My mother – who barely survived my birth – said that I was a throwback to my great-uncle Umberto – The Italian Giant, they called him. A very colorful character."

"There, you see!" cried Prudence triumphantly, "it's by no means sure that your offspring would be giants like you. But regardless of their size, how proud I'd be to bear them, to be their mother. The world needs more of you, my love."

By this time Lord John was almost swooning with emotion. "My God ... my God ..." he muttered, "but can we ... can we ...?"

"Of course we can, darling, and I think I know just how we can manage it."

"You do?"

"I've been thinking of it ... thinking of what we could do if we wanted to get together ... and I think I know how we would work it: We'd take our clothes off, of course ..."

"Of course ..."

"And then ..." she paused, then suddenly she sounded very shy: "John, do you think now's the time for us to blow the candles out?"

"Would you like that?"

Another pause, then she said, "I want what you want."

"That would be my response, too," he said. "But everything else being equal, I think I'd prefer to make love in the light ... so I can see what's going on, if you know what I mean."

"Fine!" she cried. "Good: We'll make love in the light ..." She seemed to be thinking about it, then she declared, "Yes, that's good; I want it too."

"All right," he said, "so you were saying we'd take our clothes off ..."

"Yes. And then you'd lie down, and I'd get on top of you and sort of ... impale myself on you, taking as much of you as I could manage, and at the rate I could manage, until you ... spurted your seed into me."

"Just like that?"

"Yes, I think so. And that way you needn't be afraid of hurting me ... any more than I wanted to be."

"You would *want* to be hurt?"

"Well, John, this is my first time—"

He broke in: "Mine, too."

With a smile of love, she said, gently, "I know. That's actually lovely, your being a virgin: We'll explore this together. But for me there's a difference: The first time means some pain. But that's all right, because with me on top, I can control it, I can manage it."

"You've thought this all out!"

"John, I've been *dreaming* of it ever since you proposed! Oh, I knew you were in love with Her Majesty, but I thought ... well I *hoped* ... that maybe I could make you love *me.*"

"You were the only one from the beginning," said John, really believing it was true.

"Darling!"

She removed his clothing, piece by piece, rewarding his newly revealed flesh with little kisses. And she invited him to remove hers, which he did, emulating her manner of doing it. But when he got to the half-chemise which covered her breasts, she said, "not now – maybe later." She was a statuesque woman, well formed, and she told herself that it might be better not to overwhelm her shy Lord all at once. Let the chemise come off at the right time, she thought.

John lay on the bed with his member half erect – in no condition to impale anyone. Prudence rubbed oil into her palms, and very gently began to stimulate her Lord, assuring him that this was quite usual in these circumstances. (Her position as Lady in Waiting had allowed her to pick up all kinds of helpful gossip from Her Majesty's handmaids – including the many ways one could help lovers become ready.) It didn't take very much of these attentions to make John fully engorged. She had seen his penis before, but never like the tower of strength it became under her ministrations. "Oh my God," she said, "you're beautiful! Now let's see how much of that I can take into me ..."

And she climbed aboard and straddled him, gently taking his member and rubbing it against her vulva until she felt ready. "I'm going to sit on you," she told him throatily, "and it's probably going to hurt me, but don't worry: *I want this.*" And at her own pace and pressure she continued until she gasped and took him in, causing a spurt of blood to spill down, and John to sit up. "Don't worry, don't worry," she said, "this usually happens the first time; I should have reminded you: Remember our first night together and the goat blood? Same thing, only this time the blood's all mine."

"The maids will have something to talk about, won't they?" he said.

"Let them talk. I'm yours and you're mine, and I don't care who knows it. Now lie down and enjoy yourself."

"Yes ma'am," he said, saluting. "I'll do my best to follow orders!"

She began to move up and down, feeling relieved that her pleasure was starting to supplant her initial pain. Even more pleasing to her was the look of concentration on John's face, with his lips parting, and his breath starting to come in pants. Before long, he began involuntarily to thrust upwards, and she encouraged him: "More of that please, *more*!" And he started powerfully – *purposefully* – to thrust upwards.

Seeing the man-mountain underneath her, completely in thrall to her, excited her deeply, and she ripped off her half-chemise and leaned over him. “Put your hands on me!” she ordered; he put his hands on her breasts and with a wall-shaking roar spurted deep into her welcoming darkness.

The look of him and the thundering of him as he climaxed filled her with awe and with love. She felt she might really be willing to die for him.

“I’m afraid I made a lot of noise just now,” he said when he could speak, “did you mind?”

“Mind? I loved it – it means you’re mine!” She kissed him tenderly, but he broke the kiss.

“But you didn’t climax – did you?”

“No sweetheart – not this time. But I feel more satisfied than I can tell you.”

“But I want you to climax, too!”

“I feel sure I will, soon. Maybe next time. Don’t worry, my love, it’s just going to keep getting better and better.”

“How can you be so sure?” he asked.

“With a man like you and a woman like me,” she said, “it has to happen!”

FIFTY-SEVEN

I want to be grateful.

Late at night, after the wedding banquet was over and everyone was in bed, Anna sat alone in her council room, the portrait of Andrew Steele in her hand. "What a day it has been, my love," she said. "At the Great Cathedral there was not only the baptism of little Turco, but right afterwards the wedding of Jane and Emanuel – this time *in* the Cathedral, thanks to a ruling by our new Archbishop. I think the sequence was strange – I mean logically, a wedding should normally come *before* the baptism, not after – wouldn't you think? You need the one before you can get to the other, right?

"I guess they did it that way because if you started with the wedding, the baptism might seem to be anti-climactic. But for me, the baptism was very compelling in its own right. Angelina was so beautiful – she always is – she has this glow, this radiance coming from her. Turco chose well when he chose her, but I remember that everyone sniffed. *What – a kitchen maid? How could he?* But Turco knew very well what he was doing: Lady Angelina is beautiful, not only on the outside but on the inside, as well. Turco knew better than the rest of us – he usually does.

"And Friar Anselm was there to handle the baptism. He looks very old, but he's still as sweet as ever. He did something *very sweet* – but oh! I'm getting ahead of myself! I should say first that Turco had chosen Lord Flexner as God Father. When the time came for him to recite the Profession of Faith, John was so sincere; his whole body seemed to vibrate with it. Then, after the immersion – here comes the sweet part – Friar Anselm kissed the cross he was wearing, then kissed the God Father, John, and asked John to kiss the baby, which he did. At that moment, everybody up there – the good Friar, Turco, Angelina, the little baby, and Lord John all seemed to glow with light – all of them, really! I wasn't the only one who thought so; after the service some people came up to me and mentioned that glow, and I can still feel it.

"Not that Jane and Emanuel's wedding wasn't also lovely in its way. Naturally Jane was dressed in blue – for purity, don't you know. And – judging by the way she complained about Emanuel's making her wait until after they were officially married – Jane *earned* that blue gown!

"The wedding ceremony wasn't handled by Friar Anselm but by the Archbishop – because of Jane's high rank, naturally. Of course there was the usual exchange of vows – will you take this woman, and so forth. But they added their own! Emanuel said, *For as long as I live, I will be there for you, Jane, with everything I have and with everything I am.* And she replied in kind. I tell you, Andrew: The red-hot intensity of their love has burned away whatever stain his father left on the family shield. It's an honor to know them.

"And they were so cute! During the banquet, they had eyes only for each other, and though they were very polite to all the guests who came up to congratulate them – very many well wishers, thank God – you could just tell that they could scarcely wait 'til they escaped to their bed!

"And I hope you will approve of what I thought of next: I had plenty of guards stationed all the way from the banquet room to their bedroom. I didn't want any of that pre-coital nonsense we've grown too used to around here – you know, people ripping off a part of the bride's gown for their good luck, or snatching her garter to ensure fidelity in their own marriages, or breaking into the bedroom and forcing the bride to drink a potion supposed to give her energy for a night of love! Judging by appearances, Jane certainly didn't need any such reviving potion (though by morning, poor Emanuel might)!

"Anyway, I announced that there would be no such funny business, and if they were interested in Jane's garter, or a piece of her dress, later on those items would be auctioned off, the proceeds going to charity. The guests must have thought I was joking, because when the Bride and Groom made their escape, a bunch of drunken Lords tried to follow them, only to find the Guards blocking their way. Some people are simply strange; I've given up trying to figure them out.

"And all during the banquet people kept giving me commiserating looks, as if to show me that they sympathized with my envy of Jane, and my envy of Angelina, who now have what I never can. But they're so *wrong* – I have no such envy! I'm very happy for them, and I wish them a life of complete happiness! They have their lovers, and I have you, Andrew, and what is equally important, I have a nation at this moment at peace.

"It was scary for a while, and you must know that I went through a pretty dark place; I didn't know how it might end. But thank Heaven I got out of there and got back to the light, and to the land of the living! And thank

Heaven we had just the right circumstances, and just the right people to keep disaster at bay. And I was part of that. Thanks to me – *in part* to me – thousands of people will live who otherwise might have died. I'd like to think of myself as a Queen of Life – at least I am for the moment. It might not always be this way, but if I've learned one thing, it's this: *I want to be grateful for every single day.* And even though I'm no longer able to touch your hand, dearest, I'm grateful that I'm alive and still able to love you."